A PLACE BEHIND THE WORLD

D1396426

". . . an engrossing tale, certain to touch the heart!"
CHERRY BOONE O'NEILL
Author of *Starving for Attention*

". . . a deftly crafted weaving which touches the reader in all the right places. God's redemptive love and creative ways converge in a personal pilgrimage and a private drama to produce surprise and redemption."
DAN O'NEILL
Mercy Corps International

". . . however one classifies this novel, it's a dazzling performance."
WILLIAM GRIFFIN
Publishers Weekly

". . . a page-turner to keep Christians awake at night—reading!"
JAMIE BUCKINGHAM
Charisma magazine

"David Hazard is a writer of promise and large vision. . ."
LUCI SHAW
Author of *God in the Dark*

"A marvelously creative work. Suspenseful, touching. Passed my tear-duct test."
LEONARD LeSOURD
Editor, Chosen Books

A PLACE
BEHIND
THE WORLD

A Novel by

DAVID HAZARD

WORD PUBLISHING

Word (UK) Ltd
Milton Keynes, England

WORD AUSTRALIA
Kilsyth, Victoria, Australia

STRUIK CHRISTIAN BOOKS (PTY) LTD
Maitland, South Africa

ALBY COMMERCIAL ENTERPRISES PTE LTD
Balmoral Road, Singapore

CHRISTIAN MARKETING NEW ZEALAND LTD
Havelock North, New Zealand

JENSCO LTD
Hong Kong

SALVATION BOOK CENTRE
Malaysia

A PLACE BEHIND THE WORLD

First published in the USA by Bethany House Publishers 1991.

Word (UK) Ltd. edition 1992.

ISBN 0-85009-534-4 (Australia ISBN 1-86258-198-3)

Besides the poetic fragments acknowledged in the text as the creation of E. E. Cummings, some readers may note allusions to: Walter de la Mare's "The Phantom" (p. 43); Emily Dickinson's "I felt a funeral in my brain" (p. 145); Carl Sandburg's "Little Word, Little White Bird" (p. 177); Francis Thompson's "The Hound of Heaven" (p. 178); and Gerald Manley Hopkins' "God's Grandeur" (p. 180). The poem "Two Ghosts" (pp. 133-134) is an original by the author.

Permission to quote Walter de la Mare granted by Dover Publications, Inc., New York, New York.

The lines from "somewhere I have never travelled, gladly beyond" and "All in green went my love riding" are reprinted from Complete Poems, 1913-1962, by E. E. Cummings, by permission of Liverright Publishing Corporation. Copyright © 1923, 1925, 1931, 1935, 1938, 1939, 1940, 1944, 1945, 1946, 1947, 1948, 1949, 1950, 1951, 1952, 1953, 1954, 1955, 1956, 1957, 1958, 1959, 1960, 1961, 1962, by the Trustees for the E. E. Cummings Trust. Copyright © 1961, 1963, 1968 by Marion Morehouse Cummings.

Cover illustration: Painting C Aleah Koury. Used with permission of the Artist.

Printed and bound in Great Britain for Word (UK) Ltd. by Cox & Wyman Ltd., Reading.

92 93 94 95 / 10 9 8 7 6 5 4 3 2 1

To MaryLynne

And to Aaron, Joel and Sarah Beth
"I have no greater joy than to know
my children walk in truth."

One

She crouched behind a thick copse of ferns, heart beating against her ribs. The dense autumn wilderness echoed with the voice.

Mary!

Far up the ravine, she thought there was a flicker of movement—whether coming for her or retreating, she couldn't tell. Except for the rushing thunder of the waterfall that was blowing a fine cool mist across her face, all else was still.

She wasn't sure she had actually heard a man's voice, but its echo in her mind was enough to raise a buried terror. It sounded deep and compelling—not cold exactly, but with a firmness that demanded she come out of hiding.

Ducking lower behind the ferns, she felt tense, and unable to comprehend what had happened. She'd never seen these woods or this waterfall, and had no idea how she'd come here. Scanning the autumn trees, tensing at an imagined movement or a fleeting shadow, she tried to make sense of the confused fragments floating in her mind. Like trying to sort the pieces of a broken mosaic. Only a few came together . . .

. . . of an April morning.

Making it to the ad agency through the first wave of Washington, D.C., rush hour was the least of her difficulties. At 17th Street she turned north from the greening mall, numbing herself to the certainty that things were closing in. The noon appointment in the park would determine everything.

Two copy writers and one of the other artists were early at work in the first row of office cubicles, which she successfully avoided. Passing the photo lab, she was not so fortunate.

Stanley's grinning face—the single most unwelcome sight she could imagine—thrust out of the darkroom door, with an unkempt beard, and bushy hair barely controlled in a long ponytail. Ever since he first tried to corner her, Mary had considered Stanley one of the leftover hippie types who never caught on that most women found excessive hair and unwashed clothes unappealing.

"Hey—good morning!" he said triumphantly, blocking her path. "You've been scarce around here for the last couple of weeks. I've been thinking about you."

The other women in the agency would have pushed by him without reply, because Stanley easily mistook simple politeness for encouragement. Normally, Mary couldn't find it in herself to be unkind to him, but today her control over a mounting inner chaos was too fragile.

"I'm not feeling well," she said abruptly. "Please let me get by."

Impossible to offend, he gave her his hungry-dog grin. "Take a look at this," he said, shoving an ad slick into her hands. "It's for this week's insert in the *Post*. What do you think?"

He'd sketched a pen-and-watercolor of an attractive woman in her mid-twenties, finely sculpted cheekbones, and shoulder-length blond hair being blown by a light breeze. She was looking back over her shoulder, and there was real artistry in the complicated expression of longing green eyes and slightly knit brows. A certain distress. An appeal. An unhappy secret.

The rest of the sketch was Stanley's pathetic and lonely imagination at work with a slender, athletic body in a silk teddy. But the hidden anxiety that bled through the woman's face—*Mary's* face—turned her to ice.

Stanley was oblivious to what he'd captured on paper or to her response. "So what do you think?" he repeated suggestively, edging closer.

Mary thought, but did not say, *The eyes are all wrong. They have life in them.*

She thrust the slick back at him and stepped past, all in one swift movement. "You forgot the little scar by my left eye, from falling off a horse when I was small."

"I thought you'd be flattered," he called after her, deflated. "Hey, what's with you lately? What are you involved in? Or should I ask, *who* are you involved with?"

She shut her door firmly on the grating voice.

Noon was unmercifully long in coming. By 11:45 apprehension knifed through her stomach till she bent over her crossed arms for relief. Mary slipped into flats for walking and headed south. From the agency it was only a few blocks to the small park north of the White House at Dupont Circle. Noontime traffic was picking up.

She found a bench and waited, lost to the living spring morning all around.

In the center of the circular park, the tall fountain endlessly spilled water, which caught the innocent light as it fell into the dark pool circling its base. Beside this pool, a little girl in a pink pinwale dress played with a porcelain-faced doll. Watching her brought a prick of unbearable sweetness and sorrow. Mary felt light-headed and ill. Her hands clenched tight in her lap.

Where is he? she thought desperately, her eyes darting back and forth across the lanes of speeding traffic. *Why isn't he coming? I can't take this. He needs to know the truth.*

Here, the memory fragments began to disintegrate . . .

A street flooded with cars . . . someone dashing . . . a bright flash, as of sun on glass or on water . . . a violent fall. . . .

———

"Mary!"

She had opened her eyes groggily in this thickness of woodland ferns. The traffic noise and splash of the fountain had blurred into the rush of the waterfall. Forest-scented air revived her, and she pulled in breath the way someone who has nearly drowned recovers the surface. Her entire body tingled, like an arm that's been asleep.

When she came fully awake, it was to a wild cold sky and the slant of afternoon shadows in strangely brooding trees. On the branches leaves hung in a weak November sort of light. *Why is it fall?* she wondered. Then, more frantic, *Where is the park?* Strangest of all, she was still wearing the same blouse and twill slacks, the same quilted rose jacket she'd worn to the agency—that morning? Or how long ago?

And then the dawning of terror: *The voice—the man who was calling—he must have kidnapped me from the park. But why? He must have knocked me unconscious. How did I get away?*

Her mind seemed to be working against her, throwing up a barrier to even one vital clue that would tell her exactly what had happened. If someone was stalking her, though, it was even more important to get away from here. Wherever *here* was.

For the first time, she turned her full attention to the landscape.

She was concealed in a small wooded cove at the bottom of a steep ravine. The ferns that hid her grew at the base of one of its sheer rock walls. Beyond a stone-cobbled stream rose the ravine's opposite wall, at the top of which, three sentinel evergreens guarded the edge of the precipice. Down this cliff thundered the waterfall, slicing apart on stone outcroppings and crashing into a bright pool, not twenty feet from her hiding place.

A wilderness of broken beauty—the thought flitted through her mind as she studied the strewn rocks and broken branches.

Seeing the water, a sensation of falling swept over her. And a flicker from the moment before waking . . . *white light bursting around me, like a small sun splitting the heart of a great stone, spraying me with diamonds of pain. . . .*

I must have fallen over the waterfall, she thought, realizing at once how peculiar and impossible an idea that was. *I couldn't have survived a fall like that,* she concluded, more coherently, and let the idea go.

The pool sharply narrowed into a silver brightness, coursing between the bent iron-gray trunks of hawthorn, oak, maple and mounds of brush. This brook stretched away to her right, down to where the ravine appeared to fan open.

Now that the initial shock of waking had passed, two distinct feelings fought within her.

One was a sharpened sense of wariness. Odd, at a moment like this, but it brought to mind a line of familiar poetry: *Four lean hounds crouched low and smiling . . . Paler be they than daunting death . . . the merry deer ran before. . . .* The words gave voice to her instinct—that she was not alone in this place, that the silence was alive and listening, lean and willing to wait.

The other sense at work in her was something almost the exact opposite. She felt something familiar in these woods, as if it was a place she ought to know. Its familiarity came from a certain invisible quality that hung in the air, behind the withering canopy of leaves, behind the late-season shabbiness of rhododendrons and bracken. It was an abandoned emptiness, which was beginning to invade her with a feeling she'd carried all her life—something she'd thought of as "an autumn sorrow."

In a way, meeting this sense now worked to her benefit. She was feeling less afraid and more in control. This could be the forest in a fairytale. Or in a nightmare. Whatever came next, she could handle it.

As she'd been studying the trees, the stream's cool sounds had been teasing her. She ran the tip of her tongue over cottony-dry lips. Maybe it was safe to slip out of hiding, just for a moment, for a drink.

One more glance at the trees down the ravine, and above the waterfall. Not a leaf stirred.

Creeping on hands and knees, she reached the stream's edge and, dipping her hands in the flow, drank quickly, furtively. And quite unexpectedly, found herself thinking of a long-ago moment when she'd first felt this alone, this abandoned.

Perhaps it was triggered by this strange forest— this place of unsettling moods. Or maybe it was her own image, which she now caught on the water's rippling surface, reflecting back through eyes that held wells of pain, a brief, sharp glimpse into a time long gone. She was a little girl then, no more than three years old . . .

. . . in the sunlit kitchen of a farmhouse. She wailed and clutched at the skirt of a pretty blond woman who was trying to pull free.

"Mommy has to leave now, honey, or I'll miss my plane. Be a good girl."

A hawkish-looking older woman was prying the little girl's fingers from the folds of cloth. Her nails dug into Mary's arm, and the pain made her scream and stamp her feet.

The screen door slammed. The pretty woman was gone.

A gray-haired man with kindly eyes patted Mary's head. Then he also went out the screen door, and there was the sound of a car on the gravel drive.

Mary knew her mommy was not coming back, and began to sob.

The old woman shook her. "It won't do you any good to cry. I don't like this any more than you do."

Mary screamed again, trying to wrench free and run outside.

A slap stung her face. "I won't have this, do you hear me? Not if you have to live in my house. Stop it!" . . .

. . . She blinked. The water had run through her cupped hands.

Even the painful memory helped in a way: She could draw on an old resolve, something she'd learned before she was old enough to put it into words. *To survive, you have to go it alone. Crying gets you nothing. You will never cry.*

"I'm going to find my way out of here," she whispered.

Again, her eyes traced the waterfall up the cliff. On the current of cool, loam-scented air came two unexpected odors, delicate as descending spiders' threads: the faint scent of a man's expensive cologne, and the acrid smell of diesel exhaust. At the top of the waterfall, the city park and the springtime simply were waiting for her to return!

Mystified, she stood.

"Mary! So there you are!"

Like a rabbit terrified at the crack of a rifle, she scrambled frantically around the pool's stone-littered banks.

Reaching the base of the cliff, she struggled to pull herself up onto the lowest rock ledge. Close beside her now, the waterfall's spray dampened her face and hair.

"Mary? I can hear you!" came the dreaded call.

He was coming down the side of the ravine, still concealed by the trees' shadows.

Groping at the mossy rocks overhead, her fingers slipped over the cliff's uncaring face, then met a solid crease in the stone. She dug in her fingers and struggled to pull up one ledge higher as the sounds of breaking underbrush grew nearer. Now she was many feet above the pool, the thunder of the waterfall loud in her ears. Straining upward, she saw that the cliff was smooth the rest of the way.

"You can't escape up there," the voice called again.

She glanced over her shoulder. For a split second there was no one—and then a tall figure appeared in the underbrush, moving quickly toward her through the forest's murky light.

One more futile attempt at the rock face, and she was suddenly overcome with panic. How foolish she'd been to leave herself in the open like this. *Why do I always make the wrong move?*

Turning, she pressed one shoulder against the rock to brace herself on the ledge so she could give him a solid kick if he climbed up after her.

The man emerged from the shadow-light into the open. Instead of approaching the cliff, he sat down on a spill of large stones at the far side of the pool. For a moment he watched her and said nothing. Then a satisfied grin spread across his face.

"I knew I'd flush you out if I stayed on your trail long enough."

Her heart seemed to be choking her as she looked down into the handsome, smiling face. Was it the triumph crouched inside the deep-set eyes that was so unsettling? Or just that she had stupidly cornered herself?

She felt like a doe she'd once seen struggling to death in the wire of a snare.

Two

The water churned in the pool beneath her precarious refuge.

He was dressed in jeans and a crisp navy windbreaker and sat with his arms folded across his chest, waiting.

"How do you know my name?" she demanded at last.

"Mary." He said it flatly, in the passionless tone of a collector displaying a butterfly. "It's like the word *mara*. Bitter. Isn't that in the Bible somewhere?" An odd reply. And the way he said the word *bitter* left it hanging in the air like a judgment.

He stood and moved to the foot of the cliff, taking the litter of rocks with an easy, athletic stride. Like a living sculpture. Strong, good-looking features and perfect proportions. Directly below her, he stopped. To her relief, he made no attempt to climb. Just stood there studying her.

"How do you know my name?" she asked again. "Did you bring me here?"

"You had to be Mary. Who else? I heard someone calling that name a little while ago. Didn't you hear it?" he asked. "Now I'm just trying to figure out why on earth a woman in nice clothes is trying to scale a rock wall." He ended with a chuckle.

His tone—and that disarming grin—was starting to make her less afraid and merely irritated. But there was something about his eyes that made her feel as if she were on a witness stand. She would not offer him any information.

"I don't see what's so funny," she called down.

"You don't like to think you're being laughed at, do you?" he remarked. "One of those supersensitive types."

"You said you heard someone calling my name," she said to distract him from the personal comments.

"Yes. But I don't hear anything now, do you? And you haven't told me what you're doing up there."

She didn't answer. But the man kept staring, which made Mary feel more awkward by the moment.

How do I explain? What will it sound like when I tell him I don't know where I am or how I got here? A lone and confused woman, perched on a rock ledge. How could she tell him that it was supposed to be spring in Washington without sounding like a mental case.

"You never told me your name," she began slowly.

The stranger's eyes turned mocking. "And I won't tell you either. You see, you're trying to figure out if you can trust me. But how do I know I can trust you?"

He was infuriating. Unfortunately, he had the advantage.

"I've got to get out of here," she shot back, thinking, *I'd better humor him.* "Please, can you just show me how to get out of here?"

"Sure I can show you. But we're not going anywhere until you come down."

While she was considering whether to trust this difficult man, she noticed that he was cradling his right arm. At first she'd thought his arms were folded arrogantly across his chest. Now it was evident he was favoring his right elbow, and his grin was somehow re-sketched—as if by a minor stroke of a pencil—so that it had taken on a slight twist of pain.

Like watching the subtle shift of expressions on the face of a skilled actor, whether you saw the man's expression as a mocking superior grin or as a grimace of pain depended very much on how you chose to see it.

"How did you hurt your arm?" she asked.

"Coming all the way down the steep part of the ravine to help you," he said with some testiness. "I think my elbow might be broken. So I can't climb up there and rescue you, if that's what you expect. You got yourself up there, and you'll have to get yourself down."

When she didn't budge, his expression changed again.

"You think I've come to hurt you?" he asked, all wounded dignity. His face clearly said, *So that's the thanks I get for risking my neck to help someone in trouble.*

Despite her own crisis, this actually succeeded in making her feel sorry for him. Also a touch guilty. She wanted to believe him. For all her artistic powers of observation, she'd never in her life been good at reading men. Now this stranger didn't seem at all threatening, just hurt—and all because of her.

The air coming down the cliff feathered a strand of hair. She shivered. It had become a good deal colder. *You've always been so caring,* she told herself. *In fact, too caring for your own good.*

Then, obediently, she carefully lowered herself down from the rocks.

Once on the ground, she kept her eyes riveted on him. She was relieved that he made no move toward her.

It's odd, she thought. *From the ledge he was so incredibly good-looking.* This close she could see his eyes were only vaguely blue—unsettling eyes, like those of a wild dog. She'd also misjudged his age—thinking him in his twenties—because she now could see the slight brush of gray at his temples. Still, even with these revisions, his features were appealing.

"I took a first-aid elective when I was in art school," she offered. "Maybe you should let me have a look at your arm."

He ignored this.

"I couldn't tell you this while you were up on the rocks," he whispered, his manner suddenly wary.

"You were already upset, and I didn't want you to fall. But we're in real danger if we don't get out of here. Now. You've got to follow me. Quietly as you can."

"Why?"

"Just follow me," he whispered urgently.

"Where are we going?" Mary dropped into a whisper too, his sudden change of mood throwing her off-balance again.

"I'll answer your questions as best I can. But not now. Not here. You'll understand better if I show you something first."

Still cradling his right arm, he started off into the trees, giving only a backward glance to see if she was coming. With no desire to stay behind alone, she followed him out between the widening walls of the ravine.

He kept to the mossy stream bank, which was mostly free of undergrowth, moving with caution, staying low. Then he veered to the right, away from the stream, into the deeper shadows and tangles. She went in after him, her sleeves and hair catching on tiny thorn-hooks. He was charging ahead in a confusion of brambles that rolled up all around like mounds of barbed wire, leading her straight through the worst of it.

"Wouldn't it be better to go back along the stream?" she whispered as loudly as she dared. "It was clearer there."

"Of course it's clearer," he said sharply, over his shoulder. He didn't sound cautious now, merely annoyed. Mary decided he was the most changeable man she'd ever met. He'd succeeded in making her so unsure of her own perceptions that she felt guilty for even questioning him.

"The stream runs into some open places," he explained. "That'll make it easier for him to spot us. If we get separated, stay in the thickest part of the woods at all times. You've got to remember that."

"What are you talking about? Who will spot us?"

He did not respond.

A little farther and the trees abruptly ended, opening a startling panorama.

They'd come out to a grassy meadow that sat like a shelf atop the last slope of a mountain. The stream wandered across it before starting its rushing descent, disappearing below them in another autumn wilderness. She looked out over a great bowl of forest, with trees standing shoulder-to-shoulder, guardlike, spreading for miles toward the setting sun.

Immediately that nagging sense of the familiar was back—like walking into a room she'd known all her life, only to find that the walls and floor and ceiling had exploded in all directions and it was much, much larger than remembered.

The curve of the forest sloped away from her down into the great distance. The closer forest canopy was faded yellows and oranges. After that, much of the central slope was a leathery tan, undoubtedly thick with oaks. Beyond this were scatterings of dark green—pine groves perhaps. At the lowest point, far distant, she could see nothing more than a collecting of darkness, as if the whole wilderness were focusing all of its shadows into one dusky point.

But the distant sky was what captured her attention. *It must be an illusion,* she concluded, staring at the expanse above the deepening forest. *Some kind of atmospheric condition.*

The far horizon had a heavy, gauzy appearance—thick with blues, purples, reds. It was as if the sun had dropped in back of a veil, which came down to touch the distant, collecting shadows. From behind this haze, a spectacular brightness trumpeted up and across the great cold autumn sky, igniting the clouds in scarlet and gold.

She felt as if she had come into an immense amphitheater, with arc lights shining overhead, waiting for a play to begin.

The man had not stepped into the open with her but watched cautiously from a protection of trees, occasionally glancing back into the deep shades of the ravine. "He could see you," he whispered finally, motioning her back.

She shook her head. "I'm not moving another step until you give me some answers. How far are we from Washington?"

He motioned fiercely for her to lower her voice. "We're very close to Washington."

"Where—?"

"Not another word—you've got to be quiet," he interrupted. "I think I just heard someone, back up there in the ravine."

Mary felt sick with dread. Was her unknown pursuer out there in the woods any more dangerous than this one she could see? *Even if this guy is some kind of lunatic or kidnapper,* she reasoned, *the only hope I've got is to play along and get all the information I can.*

"Please, just answer me plainly," she tried again. "Where in the world are we?"

"I told you," he replied, "we're very close to Washington—and in a way we're very far from it. Do you believe in an invisible world? A world *behind* the world?"

"Incredible," she replied, attempting to humor him. A place behind the world. Not likely. She had cried out once for just such a world. But there was no answer—and no such place.

"How did I get here?" she tried again.

"I think the only people who find their way here are great saints. Or great sinners."

Another odd answer. In case he was watching for a hint of response, she composed a look of innocence.

"We're on the other side," he continued. "This is the place of hidden things. Events that have been lost—or concealed. There's only one reason a man or woman ever comes here. Things done in secret come out here. It's a place of reckoning, Mary."

His adding her name, as though to make some inscrutable point, made her even more uncomfortable beneath the pale gaze. He must have been observing her, then, even back in Washington. How much did he really know about her?

"There's a way to get out of here," he said, his mood shifting again, lightening. "If you stick close to me, I think we can dodge him and find our way to—"

"You keep talking about 'him,'" she interrupted. "Who? Who are you talking about?"

He hesitated. "He's dangerous, like a trained hunter," he answered slowly. "That voice you heard calling you—that's him. For some reason he's stalking you. If I hadn't found you first, he would have cornered you back at the waterfall."

"So this hunter," she said, still accommodating him, "he's following me—stalking me?"

"Yes—but he's subtle. He'll draw you out of hiding by strategy, influence. Tricks. It's a mind game for him. And you're the target."

"I see," she nodded indulgently.

"All right," he flared, indignant. "If you think I'm joking, try this. I say he's looking for you because he knows something you're hiding—something you probably wish you'd never done. Am I getting warm?"

She stared at him with a constricting tightness in her chest. Did he really know about her? He was crazier than she'd thought—probably more dangerous, too.

Suddenly she focused on his right arm, which he'd been jabbing at her to make his point, and her eyes flashed.

"There's nothing wrong with your arm—not the way you've been swinging it around just now. You lied to me, didn't you?" *Another man who lies*, she thought angrily.

The boldness blanked off his face. Sheepishly he said, "All right. So I lied. I only did it to win your trust, so you'd follow me."

"Win my trust? By lying?"

"Would you have come down off that ledge if I hadn't? I don't think you trust me, even though I'm being honest with you now."

This was going to be tricky—a battleground of words.

When she didn't reply at once, he pressed her. "We can't stand here arguing. He's probably getting close. If we can stay hidden," he said, pointing vaguely off in the distance, "and get ourselves down to the—"

"I won't go anywhere with you," she broke in. "Not until you tell me who you are. And where we are—really."

His face went through another of its subtle changes, settling on glaring suspicion. "Wait a minute. I think I see what's going on here. What an idiot I've been!" He was flushed with anger now. "All this time I believed I was helping a poor lost female. But you're just pretending to be lost so I'd come out of hiding and help you." Before he could say more, a shout cut him off.

"Mary!"

Instantly she recognized the same voice that had called her earlier. Someone *was* hunting for her.

"He heard you!" the stranger said, his eyes widening. Then they narrowed. "How does he know your name, anyway? Unless you're working with him! That's it! You're a decoy, aren't you? You little traitor," he accused bitterly. Cursing, he took off at a run into the woods.

In panic, she rushed after him, but with the thick brush there was no way she could keep up. It was remarkable how quickly he vanished into the shadows. In a moment there was not even the sound of his flight.

The unfamiliar forest seemed to tighten its grip. She was alone and terrified.

Three

Moments after the stranger vanished, she heard someone moving toward her from up in the ravine.

Panic sent her plunging into the forest undergrowth, thorns again tearing at her and slowing her progress.

Then she checked herself.

Running from a maniac—? The thought stopped her in her tracks. This would never work. There was only one escape, and that was to hide.

Desperately she looked around for some thick brush to duck into until he passed. *Even better,* she thought, *if it's a place that's obvious, he won't think to look there.* At the same moment she spotted it.

At the mouth of the ravine—where her pursuer would emerge at any moment—was a stand of four or five young locust trees. Beneath them, a low weaving of wild grapevines formed a concealing thatch.

She made a dash for the trees. But she saw—too late—that the vines had lost some of their leaves, so the thatch was tattered and nowhere as thick as it looked from a distance.

A twig snapped, alarmingly near.

She stole one last, brave second to grope for a fair-sized rock. With all her might she threw it down the hill so that it thudded and rolled into the lower forest, hoping he'd mistake it for her running down below. Then dropping to her knees, she pushed her way under the vines.

Cautiously, trying to slow her breathing, she peered out, wanting to catch sight of her pursuer.

Out of the woods came a tall thick-set man she had never seen before. He moved with stealth, and something like a cautious grace, like a buck scenting the wind.

With the vines in her way it was difficult to see much of his face. *He must be wearing some kind of mottled brown and green material*, she thought. *He blends so well against the trees.*

When he was very near her hiding place, he stopped.

He seemed to be listening, focusing on the lower forest. His legs were only inches from her face. Had he fallen for the trick?

He shifted. She felt a sudden impulse to scream, and had to bite her lower lip to contain it.

A terrible moment more, and he moved on, walking into the open field some yards beyond. She shifted soundlessly to get another look at him.

Though she made out a rough growth of beard, she could not see his face or if he was carrying a weapon. He scanned the forest below.

"I know what you've done," he said suddenly in a low voice, as if talking to someone who was not there. "But you'll wish you hadn't run from me when it's all over. If you only knew what I have in mind for you."

Her flesh tingled. She watched, hardly breathing, as he continued walking across the field and finally disappeared down the mountain slope.

———

She waited a long time before creeping out from the vines. When she finally emerged and tried to stand, her legs nearly gave way. What he'd said— that he'd make her wish she hadn't run—kept circling through her mind like a dark bird of portent. She had the impression he wasn't talking to himself at all, that he'd spoken out loud for her benefit because he knew she could hear him. But if he knew she was there, couldn't he have easily caught her?

She waited some minutes longer, watching. The trees below revealed no movement beneath their mottled canopy.

What did this man want with her? What did his threats mean? And where was the other man now?

The tension had sapped all her strength. All she wanted was to find a safe place to curl up and rest. But she had to come up with a plan to survive this nightmare. Running and fear had made her mouth go dry again.

When she was confident no one was coming up the slope, she moved cautiously back to the stream, which ran along beside the trees at the edge of the flat meadow. Here, the current slowed in a sandy pool, just before its downhill rush. She dropped to her knees at its edge. Even in her wariness she couldn't help noticing how the clouds rang down their brilliance on the water, so it flowed with the shine of gem fire.

What was it about this water—the way it carried the light within it? It reminded her of something.

Maybe I can rest right here at the edge of the woods, she thought as she scooped a handful of water. *If either one of these guys comes back, I can make a quick dash for cover. This water—it's so restful. Maybe I can get my head together.*

A memory floated up to her from the liquid depths . . .

———

. . . of a May morning. For Mary, it felt like a day more wonderful than Christmas.

In the fields surrounding the farmhouse outside the little town of Walnut Level, brown sere winter grass had been rinsed green with two weeks of April rain. The front walk was yellow with forsythia and jonquils, and irises scented the air with their magic fragrance. The white cross-flowers of the dogwoods here on Maryland's eastern shore would stay tightly unresurrected for some weeks, but the first roses were holding out their buds.

It was *May*. Green, yellow, purple, pink living May.

"Are you dressed, Mary?" Uncle Oliver called up

the stairs on that first May morning.

In her room beneath the eaves, Mary was rifling her closet for something special to wear. The rooster had roused her early. From her window Mary had crayoned, in red on yellow construction paper, the barn and two outbuildings. At first she'd thought of giving it to her kindergarten teacher. But, as always, it would go to someone else. She had just decided on her white dress, the one with Aunt Lucille's needlework smocking above the blue sash, when her uncle called again, his gravelly old voice echoing up the stairwell.

"This is our morning, girl," he hollered from the bottom step. "Hurry down. There's just enough time to get out to the garden and back before Auntie Lucille wants us for breakfast. You know she doesn't take any excuses when we're late."

Mary plunged down the steps, waving her sketch. "Look what I drew, Oliver."

"Oliver" was a familiarity he allowed her when Aunt Lucille was out of earshot. Manners had their firm boundaries: all men were *sir*, all women *ma'am*. But in private Oliver kept no such distance between them.

He took Mary's paper with a flourish. Holding it at arm's length, head reared back the way he always did when he was without his glasses, he said, "Well, now, there's another masterpiece. Never knew a six-year-old could draw so good. You do have a way of looking at things. Like the way you drew my shed door hanging catty-wampus like it does. I'll hang this over my workbench with the others."

He laid the drawing on the front-hall table and cocked one elbow in Mary's direction. She slipped her hand into the crook of his arm. "Now, Lady Mary," he beamed, "something tells me there just might be a surprise for you out in the garden."

Down the porch steps they went and around the huge old magnolia in the side yard. The sky was blue, the air smelled clean. The sun had not yet risen above the distant woods where Oliver used to hunt ring-necked pheasant before age caught up with him.

Toward the garden they headed, "Lord Oliver" walking stiffly, with "Lady Mary" skipping at his side.

Mary had a dim idea of why her Uncle Oliver created this fantasy of grandness for her. Not long ago she'd come downstairs early one morning and overheard Aunt Lucille scolding him in the kitchen.

"We cannot afford such extravagance."

"Someone's got to make it up to the poor little thing," Oliver insisted. "Someone's got to make a life for her."

Somehow Mary understood that she was "the poor little thing" who needed to have a life made for her.

Aunt Lucille objected, "When we agreed to raise your niece's child, it was with the understanding that her mother and her *paramour* would help with the support. So now he's disappeared, as if we didn't know he would, and she's decided to stay on the west coast 'to forget the mistakes of my youth and start my life over.' " Aunt Lucille rolled off this last comment in the high, sing-songy voice she often used when repeating something she'd heard the pastor's wife say.

"How convenient for her," she continued bitterly. "Meantime, we haven't seen a penny. Sometimes I wish we could forget her sad mistakes—"

"Lucille!" said Oliver severely.

"Well," she answered, modifying her tone a little, "at least you don't have to go out and waste our money ordering extravagant trinkets. And without even asking me," she finished.

"Mary is my grandniece," Oliver had replied in his that-settles-it manner.

Arm in arm with Oliver now, Mary stepped carefully across the dirt drive, not wanting to scuff her black patent-leather shoes.

On the large side lawn, Oliver had built a long rose bower—a delicate tunnel of lattice and new blossoms that led them from the yard into an oblong of enormous old holly trees he had planted long ago as a young man. Outside this leafy enclosure, near the barn, was the produce garden he worked with Aunt Lucille. But inside, this seclusion of benches, birdbaths and flower beds was Oliver's realm alone. Out of this kingdom of color and fragrance, he kept the farmhouse bouqueted—from the front hall table and the kitchen sideboard up to Mary's room—with irises and jonquils in spring, a profusion of roses and dahlias through summer, and mums long after the first frost.

From the top of the tallest holly, a mockingbird marked his territory with exuberant singing.

"Now," said Oliver, once they were in the garden, "if you look hard enough you might find a surprise."

Mary seized two of his fingers and tugged impatiently. "I'll never find it by myself. You have to help!"

Oliver winced a little but chuckled, "My arthritis, child. Just let me sit here on this bench. I'll tell you when you're getting warm."

So began the game, with Mary giggling as she moved deeper into the garden, poking behind the iris blades, probing around the stone lady who reflected her Grecian beauty into a shallow pool of lilies; and with Oliver seated on the bench, calling, "Cold—warmer—no, you're getting cold again."

On went the search, as the sun's soft slow foot moved along the pathway of crushed oyster shell, finally igniting the ornamental plum tree into a fireworks of pink at the heart of the garden. At last she spied the small white-ribboned package sitting out in plain sight on a low stone wall.

She tore off the bow and wrapping paper in one motion. Opening the tiny gray-velvet case, she lifted out the surprise—a thread-like golden chain bearing a single white pearl, its iridescent depths dazzling in the sun.

Mary laughed delightedly. Charging at Oliver, she thrust the necklace into his hand. "Put it on!" she implored, dancing up and down in excitement.

"Oh, I don't believe it goes very well with this old work shirt, do you?"

"Put it on *me,* silly!" she giggled.

There was a little fumbling at the back of her collar while Oliver's stiff fingers worked the tiny clasp. Then he smoothed her fine golden hair in place.

Mary tucked her chin to her chest and, looking down, could just see the pearl resting perfectly against the smocking of her dress.

When she lifted her head, she saw tears in Oliver's eyes, and this caused a small pang in her own heart.

"What's wrong, Oliver?"

"Nothing," he whispered.

He pulled a hankie out of his back pocket and blew his nose. "How could anything be wrong on a sweet morning like this?"

She threw her arms around his neck. Sun sifted in rose-gold through the lily pool. In this moment out of time, an eternity of love passed from one to the other.

Oliver wiped his eyes again and cleared his throat.

"We'd best get back inside for breakfast now."

On the way to the house, Oliver teased her with things like, "You must let me borrow your new necklace. I'd love to wear it to the volunteer firemen's social." And, "You look like a ballerina on top of a music box."

Mary, caught up in the frivolous mood, grew giddy with laughter. She spun around on the slippery leather soles of her shoes—three, four, five dizzying spins. Then fell in a giggling heap on the lawn.

Oliver helped her up. and she darted on ahead of him, back across the driveway, up the porch steps, and followed·the faint scent of cinnamon and oatmeal inside.

"Auntie Lucille," Mary called, bursting through the swinging door into the kitchen. "Look what Uncle Oliver gave me!"

Aunt Lucille turned from the stove and, for a split second, stood with her stirring spoon in mid-air as she eyed the necklace with a smile that was void of any brightness. In the next instant, she spied something else. Her eyes flared. A sharp and horrified little shriek escaped her lips.

"Look what you've done!"

Mary froze. What was Auntie Lucille so upset about? She looked down at the front of her dress where her aunt's gaze burned. Then she saw it. On the right side of her dress, where she'd fallen on the dewy lawn, was a bright green smudge of grass stain and a brown streak of dirt.

Lucille threw down her spoon and flew across the kitchen, her talons extending.

Seizing the shoulders of Mary's dress, she began yanking it off over her head, shouting, "Take this off at once, you thoughtless, undeserving child! After all the trouble I went through making such a pretty white dress, you throw yourself in the dirt with it. It's stained. Do you understand? Ruined!"

As she pulled the dress roughly over Mary's head, Aunt Lucille snatched a fistful of the girl's hair. And, along with the sharp pain, Mary felt the delicate gold chain catch on her collar and snap. It dropped onto the linoleum at her feet, broken. She burst into tears.

By this time, Oliver had come through the swinging door, looking bewildered. "Lucille!" he commanded. "Get a hold of yourself! What on earth is the matter?"

"*This* is the matter!" she hurled back, shaking the stained dress in his face.

Then she pushed past him, through the door and out of the kitchen, complaining loudly as she stormed down the basement stairs to her laundry room. Only fragments slipped through the still-swinging door: "ruins everything she puts her hand to" and "didn't ask for her in the first place."

As Oliver sank to his knees on the linoleum, he put his arm around the child and retrieved the pearl necklace. Mary buried her face in the shoulder of his flannel shirt and held on to him.

"There, there," Oliver said, hugging her to his chest. "Only the clasp is broken. I'll take it by the jeweler's soon as I can. Come on now, my princess. I can make it good as new."

Mary hugged his neck, sobbing and sobbing. . . .

———

. . . She stared at the watery light—not in her uncle's lily pool, but in the stream in this frightening lost wilderness. Her back hurt from bending over so long. But there was a deeper, unforgotten pain.

Oliver had gotten the pearl necklace fixed. But that winter he suffered a stroke. For three gray months his eyes and thoughts grew more and more unfocused. She'd thought that if only she could hold his blue-veined hands long enough, he would sit up and squeeze her in his arms again. But Aunt Lucille would not allow her too close to him. Hadn't she caused enough trouble already?

Another spring never came for Lord Oliver and Lady Mary. Her prince, her protector, passed on to another land without her.

And she was left behind on a lonely farm, with nothing but the solemn unhappiness of her begrudging aunt.

Then the pearl necklace, the one beloved treasure that still bound her to Oliver, disappeared. She thought she saw it once, dangling at the neck of Aunt Lucille's godchild. But there was nothing she could say or do.

"Oliver," she whispered now, clinging to the memory of him and their perfect May morning.

"Only you would understand, Oliver. Only you would still love me. How I need you! I'm more lost than I've ever been in my life."

Four

From the high late-day brightness of the sky, one small reflected ray of copper light made its way inside the blind of hemlock branches. She'd crawled inside to hide and rest while deciding what to do next. The ray fell like a glowing coin on the back of her left hand. Lying on her back, she felt drowsy, as if she were sinking down and down like a fish that has ceased fighting the current of a great river.

All her life she'd felt a deep weariness inside. A kind of oldness.

As she looked at the point of light touching her hand, it occurred to her vaguely that maybe these memories were part of the mystery of where she was and what was happening to her . . .

Light . . . weariness . . . the past . . . Her eyes drifted shut . . .

. . . In the woods near the farmhouse Mary had discovered a secret place of refuge. A tree, fallen in a winter storm, rested beside a low spot where water had gathered in a small, permanent pool. It was secluded and lonely there. But peaceful. An escape from Aunt Lucille's fluctuating moods of indifferent cold or accusing fire.

Mary could lie along the trunk and dangle her hand in the water. The pool, shallow with a leafy bottom, reflected back the colors of the sky and the green-eyed little girl who stared back at her.

What was this hollow feeling that wasn't hunger and that would not go away? No longer just abandonment, but a feeling that she was searching for something. Sometimes she felt so empty, as if the wind could blow right through her ribs.

At Oliver's funeral the minister had called the world "a vale of tears." Mary thought he was saying "a *veil* of tears"—and her childish imagination pictured a gauzy curtain made of tears and drowning her in a vague sorrow.

I want you to come back for me, she pleaded, staring beyond her watery reflection into Oliver's imagined face. She would always remember him as he looked that last time he'd knelt to tuck her in and pray beside her bed: Even through clouds of weariness and age, an unquenchable spark of love lighted his eyes as he looked at her. *You're the only one who was good to me,* she longed to tell him now. *I promise I'll never love anyone besides you.*

Oliver's face receded, and from the water the child's face stared at her again, eyes now vacant with sorrow. Bits of a poem he had often read at bedtime, holding her on his lap as he underscored the lines with one stiff old finger, whispered through her mind. It was about a little girl of long ago, wandering through a cold, gloomy house by candlelight, coming upon her own reflection in a clouded mirror:

"In the dim solitude her heart remembers tearlessly. . . . Now in the dark glass she sees . . . a phantom face . . . reflecting phantom fears."

A slight breeze disturbed the waters, and the woodland air breathed its sorrow for the little figure on the edge of the pool. . . .

———

. . . She opened her eyes beneath the hemlocks and stared at the crisscrossed branches above her. How much time had passed? An hour—or two?

Then a peculiar detail caught her attention. Her hands remained folded and still across her stomach—and the point of light on top of her left hand had hardly moved.

She realized she had no idea how much time had passed since she'd awakened at the foot of the waterfall—whether part of an afternoon, or a whole day. Something was not normal about the way time moved in this place.

She sat up, alarmed. "What am I doing, lying around sleeping?" she whispered to herself. "I can't let them catch me off guard."

Shaking hemlock needles from her hair and jacket, she went back to the edge of the field and cautiously checked the lower forest again. Apparently the hunter had been outmaneuvered, because he hadn't returned to look for her. *He prob-*

ably thinks he's driving me ahead of him, out into the open.

She looked around, trying to decide what to do. *I could go back to the waterfall,* she thought. That was where she had started out in this strange new place, and maybe there she could locate some clue about how to get back to her own world.

She set off uphill. Instead of sticking to the center of the ravine, along the stream, she veered away from it to her left. With a little effort, she came to a rock outcropping along the forest floor where the cliff began its ascent.

Shortly, she was clambering along the ravine's north wall and was soon out on a tree-lined ledge. Looking back over the western vista confirmed her suspicions about time. The high trumpets of light still spanned the sky, scarcely changed at all.

Something did change, however, as she climbed higher. The air became cooler and she had to pull her quilted jacket more snugly around her. It had been fine for an April morning, but now the strong gusts of wind, each one bringing down a hail of leaves, chilled her fingers and face.

"I should be able to hear the waterfall by now," she murmured to herself, chafing her hands together. Yet she heard nothing but the wind and the sound of her own footsteps on cold-ringing stone.

A little higher and she came out on another ledge. The icy wind was so bitter she had to protect her face with her hands. Directly across, on the opposite wall of the ravine, stood the three sentinel evergreens she had seen from below.

But nothing could have prepared her for the rest of this scene.

Everything here above the falls had frozen solid—every twig and blade was crystallized in icy perfection. Even the waterfall had stiffened like folds of hung glass. A cold wall of air moved slowly, massively toward her, locking everything in this deathly frost, turning it into a pale still-life.

Beyond the trio of now-frozen evergreens—and this was the most shocking sight of all—she could see the small park at Dupont Circle, with its fountain and benches, grass and flowers, the encircling traffic. Just as she remembered it. Except that everything was hoary with ice, frozen in time. The fountain's sculpted column was white-coated; shoppers were glazed mannequins posed mid-stride on slicked sidewalks; drivers were iced at the wheels of unmoving cars. One vehicle stood at an odd angle in the street, the driver's face startled by something at the moment of freezing.

On the near side of the traffic circle, where there should have been sidewalk and buildings, this ice-coated forest began, the pavement graduating from cement into an icy stream flowing over this wilderness waterfall.

By now the moving glacier of icy wind was pushing her so hard that she stumbled back down the ridge the way she'd come. She looked back hastily at the freezing wall. Below the falls, half the pool was glassy with ice, while half still churned freely, and the surrounding trees showed only the slightest withering from the frost's advancing edge.

As she retreated to the open field again, upset and confused as she was, some mosaic pieces were fitting into place.

At least in one point, she decided, the stranger in the windbreaker was not crazy after all. Washington was not far away. Yet somehow she had found her way into some other place—a place behind the world. That knowledge seemed almost worse than the earlier uncertainty.

"A place of reckoning," he'd said. What was that supposed to mean? That she was somewhere between earth and hell? Was someone going to punish her for one mistake—after all the terrible things she'd had to struggle against in her life? Dumped by a mother she hadn't seen since she was three. Left on an isolated farm with a foul-tempered old woman, after the one person she loved was taken away. Not to mention everything since then.

Coming back to the immediate predicament, she concluded, *Obviously I can't get out the way I came in. It's like everything in the past is frozen just the way I left it. Whatever I did to get in here, I can't undo by going back that way.* It was strange how she could clearly remember everything about her life—except the last few moments in Dupont Circle.

Another sobering thought: Maybe everything she'd done in the past was still frozen behind her somewhere—each event in the stream of her life, like a witness for or against her.

She rearranged her thoughts to block out past images that were fighting to escape into her mind.

It was better never to remember certain things.

"What I want to know," she muttered angrily, "is why the wrong person always has to suffer, while the rats get away with everything."

The upper half of the mountain was now fully engulfed in crystalline whiteness. By the split in the trees where the ravine began, she could determine the exact position of the ledge where she'd stood staring in astonishment at her own world. Trees well below the ledge were now glazed.

The cold is a few hundred yards closer, she guessed. *Soon the whole ravine's going to be locked in.*

Behind her, the glacial wind-wall crept steadily down. Even if she made it through the lower forest, where in some silent grove the hunter could be waiting, how would she find a way to escape him and the wilderness?

An old feeling of entrapment made her grit her teeth. She hated having no choice.

If there's a way out, she thought determinedly as she stared at the forest below, *I'll find it.*

It was an easy hike down the final slope. When she reached the bottom, though, her new plan seemed much less promising.

Here the trees were slightly bent, as if beneath the weight of the sky, which showed some signs of late afternoon. The branches overhead webbed their limp and fading leaves together so the woods was a conspiracy of shadows. The undergrowth looked even more strangled with vines and thorns than had the mountain forest.

It's amazing, she mused, as she had in the past while doing outdoor sketches, *how fresh and alive a forest looks in summer, and how forbidding it can become in the fall.*

There was only one path, beginning where the stream flowed into the dismal woods beneath hawthorn and maple, wild cherry and red birch, all blighted-looking with the fall. Following the stream would be her best chance. But the north bank, where she was standing, was walled with thorn bushes, while the opposite southern bank looked clear. Fortunately, just where she was standing some large stones formed a natural footbridge across the water.

The stranger had told her to avoid the stream because it would bring her out into the open, and she should keep to the thickest parts of the forest. "Thanks for the great advice," she muttered, "and for leaving me on my own."

There wasn't much of a choice, really. The ice wall would be here soon, closing off the path into the ravine.

She crossed the stream, cautiously looking this way and that for any sign of pursuit.

If the frozen upper forest had a sad feeling, the lower was somber and depressing. The forest floor continued its ever-downward pitch, and before long the place where she'd entered had shrunk to a mere dot of light when she looked back. Her quick footsteps were silenced by the moss-covered path along the bank.

Once or twice, a faint scratching sound or a rustle disturbed the coffining quiet. If she stopped to listen, the sound ceased. Beside her, the stream tried to chatter a friendly slate-slap, still carrying in its depths a faint, dissolving light.

There is the same brightness in the pool at the waterfall, she mused. But back there, with so much light ringing down from the sky, it was only natural. In here, where the light was dim, it was very strange.

Where is the light coming from in all this gloom?

She realized too that in some way this water-light was helping fend off a weight of depression that was trying to sink over her.

Just around the next bend the stream slowed and deepened into another pool, like the one in the mountain meadow. Stopping at its edge, she stooped, curious, and scooped at the surface with a cupped hand. One clear drop ran down her wrist, and the tiny pool resting in her palm made her think of the morning sky before a storm—the pretty blue of lapis with an amber tiger's-eye dissolved in it.

Small rivulets escaped her fingers, falling and rippling the surface of the pool, scattering more tiger's-eye clouds. Where did her own clouds come from? When did the pain first take hold?

The ripples died away, and the surface smoothed into another image . . .

. . . In late October of the year that Oliver passed on—Aunt Lucille would never allow Mary to say "died"—Uncle Wallace began coming to stay at the farm for a week at a time. Sometimes longer.

Uncle Wallace was the youngest of Aunt Lucille's four brothers, and he'd never married. By October, when most of his small truck farm was plowed under for the season and all but a few of the migrant workers had gone south again, he was free. He came to put up storm windows, split wood and help Aunt Lucille "winterize" the farm.

That first year he also came with a wink and a gift box for Mary. With a thin-lipped nod, Aunt Lucille allowed her to accept it.

Inside the tissue paper was a beautiful doll in a Victorian outfit of deep red organdy. Her porcelain face was serene and perfect, and from one delicate hand dangled a parasol.

Mary threw her arms around Uncle Wallace's neck and kissed his cheek. He smelled of spiced cologne. "She's the most beautiful, beautiful, *beautiful* lady I've ever seen!"

He gave her an extra hard squeeze and patted the seat of her denims. "That's my girl."

Pressing her new treasure to her shirtfront, carefully, Mary ran up the stairs to her room.

From below, she heard Aunt Lucille sternly reminding her brother, "You spent too much money. And girls who are seven, soon to be eight, shouldn't be encouraged to play with dolls."

Mary heard Uncle Wallace reply that since he had no children of his own to spoil, she ought not deny him the pleasure.

Uncle Wallace was the new smile of sunlight to Mary. But there were moments, like on the long, cool evenings when he insisted she snuggle beside him on the big porch swing, when she felt there was something unhappy about him. It was more than the sorrowful tunes he whistled. It was more than the stories he told of having to work so hard on his daddy's farm, as a young man, and of several young ladies for whom he'd bought so many pretty things, only to have them "jilt" him. Sitting at his side, Mary sensed in him a loneliness like her own.

"Promise your Uncle Wallace something, Mary," he said one October evening, wrapping an arm around her shoulder. "It's a terrible thing to hurt somebody. So promise me that when a man's good to you, you won't ever hurt him—will you?"

She wasn't quite sure what he meant. But he was so good to her. His arm felt so safe around her shoulder, and it was almost as if Oliver had been given back to her. She said, "I promise, Uncle Wallace."

"That's good," he said distantly, staring into the autumn dusk. "You just do like I tell you, and you'll be fine."

The second year, Uncle Wallace arrived one autumn afternoon when Aunt Lucille was out. Mary followed him as he lugged his suitcase upstairs to the small guest room under the eaves.

"Come on in here, girl," he called. "Let me have a good look at you."

When Mary went in, he was seated on the extra dining room chair Aunt Lucille kept up there. He surprised her by hooking the belt loops on her jeans with his fingers and pulling her astride one knee. Mary resisted.

"Aw, c'mon," he said, smiling. "You're not too big for a horsy ride."

Uncomfortable and embarrassed, Mary tried to struggle free. But he gripped her arms tightly. "You don't want to fall off and hurt yourself now, do you?"

As the years passed and Uncle Wallace came to Walnut Level more frequently, something about his visits began to feel inescapable. He was good to her, lavishing money on her at county fairs. He drew her heart out to him. Then he would be distant. When she talked about a schoolboy she liked, he found fault. He began to surround her. Confuse her. Cloud out her light.

In November of the year Mary turned twelve, Uncle Wallace insisted she walk the fence line with him one day while he checked it for breaks. The walk took them far from the farmhouse and along the woods. It was warm for a late-fall day, and the air smelled of decaying leaves.

They came upon the long-abandoned tenant house, sagging so heavily beneath wild ivy and honeysuckle that it looked as though it was being dragged off its foundations.

"Do you believe in magic?" Uncle Wallace asked.

He'd been unusually quiet.

"Yes," said Mary, to be agreeable. "Sort of."

"There's leprechauns in this old place. Want to take a look?"

"Aunt Lucille told me never to go in there," she answered, "because of copperheads and broken glass and rusty nails."

He snorted. "There's no snakes. I've been in there myself a million times. C'mon. Leprechauns live here. If we're real quiet, you can see 'em. Don't you want to see leprechauns? Or maybe you're getting too 'big' to spend a little time having fun with your uncle."

He paused at the doorway, looking back. "You gonna go inside with me or not?"

This is silly, she thought. An adult trying to act like a child. Couldn't he see she was growing up? "Okay," Mary gave in, reluctantly.

She followed him in through the doorless entryway. Shards of glass and rusted cans littered the floor.

"It's dirty," she said, feeling uneasy. "Let's go."

Uncle Wallace held one finger to his lips and whispered, "No. Let's hide and watch for a little while. See if we can spot those leprechauns. I know just the place."

He took her hand, too tightly, and guided her up the dilapidated stairs to what probably had been a bedroom. On the dirty wooden floor, amid broken plaster, lay a headless plastic baby doll. In one corner was a door—a few planks of wood nailed together—opening into a large dark space under the eaves.

"In here," Uncle Wallace nodded. The smile was gone from his eyes.

Mary tried to pull her hand away. "No. I don't want to go in there."

"I've been good to you, Mary," he said, grabbing her wrist. "Now you be good to me."

She screamed.

"Shut up and do what you're told!" he shouted, shaking her. Dragging her inside, he wrestled them both in under the eaves and pulled the door closed. Only a dim light seeped through cracks in the door planks. Dust and the smell of mold filled her nose. For a moment Mary had no idea what was happening.

And then she did know.

She would never forget.

Not with the smell of dirt and spiced cologne clinging to her no matter how much she washed herself later. Not with the weight of pain crushing her heart. Not with Uncle Wallace's accusing voice echoing in her head, "You *wanted* to go in there. Just remember that."

After a full month under his forbidding stare, when he was gone, Mary fought down her shame and told Aunt Lucille.

"You're nothing but *bad blood*!" her aunt flared. "Don't you ever accuse my family of something so filthy. And don't ever speak to me about it again."

But Uncle Wallace's visits stopped.

And Mary was left with the confusing idea that she was wrong for giving in to him—and that she was guilty of something terrible, from which she could never be free, never be clean.

Five

The creeping frost breathed through the trees, calling her back from the past.

I've been moping here too long, she thought, irritated with herself.

Standing, she locked away her memories once more. The dim daylight, filtering down through the trees, had lost its copper brightness and was now pewtering the leaves of the low bushes. This interminable day was getting on after all, toward dusk. But how much time did she have before dark? She tried not to think about night overtaking her.

Then, through a break in the undergrowth, something caught her eye. In the distance, away from the stream, was an unmistakable open brightness.

A way out? Not likely, since she was, perhaps, not even halfway through the woods.

It has to be a clearing, she decided. If nothing else, a little opening would be a welcome break from these claustrophobic trees and shadows.

Leaving the stream behind, she stepped through walls of thorns into a pathway that led roughly in the direction of the light. The going was miserable at first. Sometimes the path all but disappeared when she ran up against mountains of wild rose and bindweed. She found, however, that if she persisted, a way always opened in the viney concealment, allowing her to pass. Picking her way like this, she made slow progress.

There was no doubt about it—the forest on this side of the stream opened up the farther she went. Soon the thorns thinned out and the walking became easier. She could move cautiously and make almost no noise at all.

The small clearing ahead was surrounded by hillocks of low-growing shrubs. She was close enough now to tell that the light was not coming from the sky, as she'd thought, but from the center of the clearing itself—a radiance that poured out into the woodlands as she approached.

Just the presence of this light, rinsing away the trees' dismal gloom, made something in her leap with hope. There was also, however, a stark quality to this light. The gray branches looked more severe and crooked, every imperfection exposed.

Careful, she cautioned herself as she angled quietly, secretly from one stand of bushes to another.

Closer to the clearing, the light was more fiercely penetrating. The bare branches of tulip poplars turned fluorescent, limbs casting wild shadows. The whole woods was a study in sharp angles of black and white, so that it was like walking along a country road at twilight and being caught in the headlights of an oncoming car. The light became so dazzlingly bright and the shadows so contrasting that twice she nearly lost her footing, and had to shield her eyes with one hand.

Getting down on all fours in the forest litter, she covered the last distance in a crawl, her heart beating hard. Now more than curiosity was drawing her—an appeal, mysterious and strong.

Just outside the clearing behind a low hedge, she reached up to part some branches—and stopped, amazed at what she held in her fingers. These were blueberry bushes, and beneath the rounded green leaves were small clusters of blue, juicy-looking fruit. How could these bushes be lush with life when everything else was withered and dead?

Nothing was making sense. Cautiously, she parted the branches to look inside the clearing. From its center, just above the leaf-strewn ground, there shone a small white sun. Not cold white, though, for it radiated a spectrum of colors out of its sharp halo.

Her eyes squinted shut against the brilliance, but even so she saw *him*. Standing before the light, almost in its white heart, was the strong-built form of the hunter.

When her eyes were more adjusted to the brightness she could see that he had moved away from the center. By shielding her eyes with one hand, she could see that he had sat down with his back against a tree, just a few yards from her. She recognized him first by his clothing, which, in the tricky light, seemed to pick up the swirling colors. From this angle, she could add only a few more details to her earlier impressions: a broad beam of shoulders, thick forearms, and large rough-looking hands. She could see nothing of his face, though.

Now she heard faint words, as if he were speaking in a low, measured tone. Was he talking to her or was someone else there in the clearing with him, made invisible to her by the light?

Edging silently along the hedge, she repositioned herself to get a clear view of the hunter, arguing with herself at the same time. *What do you expect a dangerous man to look like? He's going to hear you.* Carefully, she parted another blueberry bush.

But the intense light was like those powerful lanterns neighboring farm boys back on the eastern shore had used to mesmerize and poach deer at night. Shining directly on the man's face, it blurred the definition of his features, leaving her with only impressions: There was something untamed and unpredictable, and the confidence of a man who knew his way through a wilderness. If he were not dangerous, she might even want his protection.

Maybe I should quit this stupid hide-and-seek. I'm going to stand up right now and say, "Look, I'm lost in these woods and I need your help," she reasoned. *If he really wanted to hurt me, why did he call out my name back in the ravine, instead of sneaking up on me?*

While she knelt there debating about what to do, words began to form faintly in her mind, words with a delicate, ballad-like musicality to them:

. . . in his hands, the killing frost. . . .

Where he walks, the ground is red—a trail of blood. . . .

Strange phrases. Where were they coming from? She stole another look at the hunter. He sat completely still.

She will run before her hunter . . . faltering like a doe at dawn. . . .

Some inner urge seemed to compel her now to step out of hiding. Why was she playing this silly game?

He will seek her in the dark heart . . . of her wild and haunted places. . . .

Suddenly the handsome face of the first stranger came to mind, his warning rushing back: *"He's subtle. Dangerous. He'll draw you out by influence . . . mind games."*

Sharply aware that some strong agency was trying to work its way over her, these words— whether her own tired wish to give up or from something, somewhere outside her—were making her want to surrender to the hunter.

And then the accumulated distrust of a lifetime rushed in. Trusting men had always gotten her into trouble, let alone this man . . . *a trail of blood* . . . How could she even have considered—?

The berry branch slipped suddenly from her fingers.

At the noise, the hunter, alert, rolled up onto

one knee. Keenly peering at the bushes around the clearing. Listening for the smallest rustle.

Prickles shot up her back. If she bolted in fear, he could easily run her to ground. *And that's what he wants me to do,* she thought. She could almost feel his instincts at work.

In a swift movement, he rose to his feet and the light flared.

It was ridiculous, but she ducked and buried her face in her hands, as if that would hide her.

A terrifying scrunch of footsteps in leaf litter. A pause. And for an infinite moment, a listening silence.

A whispering voice inside urged: *There's no use running. Put yourself at his mercy.*

She fought against the thought and the peculiar force at work here. She hated this man for tormenting her, and she would not surrender to anyone.

Footsteps again in the leaves. Retreating? She found the courage to lift her head.

The hunter was gone.

So was the light. Once more, the trees were dusky and undefined.

Cautiously, she looked about. *This has to be a trap. He's hiding somewhere nearby, trying to get me to follow.* She'd acted like an exposed, frenzied beetle grubbing for cover in the rotting leaves. For that, she hated him.

For a long time she waited, watching. Clearly, he had gone, though. If someone else had been in the clearing, he must have gone, too.

Now that she was beginning to feel safe again, something about the woods was changing—or maybe it was only her *sense* about it. Still cautious, she stepped out into the clearing.

Beneath a vault of branches she entered a mysterious and uplifted sort of atmosphere, like arriving too late at a quiet chapel where some joyful event has just taken place. She felt as if she had missed out on something wonderful.

The feeling slipped away, however, and a faint coolness in the air was all that remained, reminding her now that by coming here she'd sidetracked her own escape from the freezing wind. Behind her, the ice wall must be gaining.

Even if it is clearer on this side of the forest, she decided stubbornly, *I'm going back to the other side.*

And, as if hurling a challenge at the hunter, she thought, *I won't make it easy for you. If you want me, you'll have to come and get me.*

She was turning from the blueberry hedge where she'd been hiding, when something caught her eye.

Only a few berries clung—dried, puckered and black—to the bare twigs.

———

On her way back to the stream, as she expected, the thorny blockade grew tighter. One part of her argued that she should have stayed where the forest was clearer. Heavy with fatigue, she had been wrestling over the two strange men. Both of them frightened her—the hunter and the handsome stranger, as she thought of them now. If this was some otherworldly place, then who were they? Angels of judgment, or hounds from hell? Or maybe this really was a bad dream, after all—and these two were only nightmarish figments of her imagination. *If it is a dream*, she thought, looking down at her leaf-strewn clothes, *it's the most real one I've ever had.*

She decided that, for now, she did not want to know. Getting out of this wilderness, whatever it meant, was the all-important thing.

Now she was back to the stream path, where the steadily cooling air had begun to raise small swirls of mist on the water's surface. The forest seemed darker.

I've got to keep moving to stay ahead of the wind, she told herself. Weariness argued. *Maybe just a short rest.*

The forked roots of a huge old beech tree had captured a cushion of yellow leaves. A comfortable place to settle, with her head wearily resting on the crook of one arm.

Beside her on the stream, wispy phantoms of fog paired and spun, like bright figures sliding over a dance floor.

How odd, she thought. *The fog is as bright as the water.* The swirling lights reminded her of the light she'd just seen in the clearing . . .

. . . *Oliver waved to her from a high mountain meadow, silhouetted against intense sunlight. She wanted to climb up to him, but held back.*

And in that instant of hesitation, he was gone.

It was a dream she had often, and it was always the same. She would wake, a hollowness inside and a deep longing she did not understand. A hunger to be known, a feeling of missing out on something or someone, mixed with dread and even resentment. A longing to be loved . . .

. . . Shortly after Uncle Wallace's last visit, Aunt Lucille took Mary for a medical checkup.

The doctor happened to be the father of Mary's best friend, Olivia. He'd also been Mary's Sunday school teacher for several years—one of those coincidences that happen to folks who live near a small country town. He was a big man with the kindest brown eyes and a bushy mustache that could never conceal his comforting smile.

It felt odd to be in his examining room, to have him so close she could feel his warm, minty breath as he checked her eyes and ears. Odd, to have him probe her stomach for pains and lumps with the same fingers that arranged flannelgraph pictures of the Lord and His disciples.

He, too, seemed to sense that in this circumstance a certain polite distance should remain as a curtain drawn between them. He excused himself and had his nurse continue the most personal part of the exam.

It was over quickly, and when Mary was dressed again, he came in and sat on the edge of the green vinyl examining table beside her. He was not "the doctor" now, but once again Olivia's father.

"Your Aunt Lucille was concerned about you for some reason, Mary. She was pretty agitated when she made the appointment last week. Beats me as to why. You're healthy as can be."

Mary smiled nervously and avoided his eyes.

He was quiet for a few moments, then said, "Mary, is something bothering you?"

Her face warmed in a blush.

"My wife says you haven't been yourself lately. She says you haven't come over to ride the ponies with Olivia."

Mary stared at her hands, growing warmer, feeling a pinch in her throat.

"You really miss your Uncle Oliver, don't you?" he ventured.

A liquid warmth filled her eyes.

"I know this doesn't take away the hurt, Mary, but you and I both know he's in a good place. I never met a man with as much compassion as your uncle. A good man. With real faith. You know you'll see him again one day. That's the promise and the hope we have."

He wrapped one huge arm around her thin shoulders, unaware that this would unleash a conflict of feelings inside her.

At his strong touch, she imagined herself a fairy-tale princess, cherished and sought by handsome suitors—good men who protected her from Uncle Wallace. And yet . . . To keep the tears from spilling down her cheeks, Mary forced her eyes wide.

"I guess your aunt is a tough old bird to live with," Olivia's father was saying. "She does care about you in her own way, even if she's hard on you. That's the way her generation was raised to be. So if you want to talk—about girl things and such—you know you can come to Olivia's mom. She said to be sure I told you that.

"And Mary," he said, dropping his arm, "if ever you need anything else, you can come to me."

He stood and, mechanically, Mary got up to leave. Olivia's dad was a good man; he had hinted at a special plan for her next birthday. His wife was good, too. And so was Olivia. But Mary was different—not like them.

Just before she stepped out of the examining room, Olivia's dad stopped her, laying his large gentle hand on hers. Whenever he did that, she felt she wanted something from him—but had no clear idea what it was.

"Are you sure there's nothing you want to talk to me about, Mary?"

His face was so kind as he waited for her reply. But if she told him the truth, he would know how ugly and horrible she was. If he knew, would he still care about her?

"No, nothing," was all she could say.

———

On Mary's thirteenth birthday, Olivia's father led her out to the running shed on their farm. Olivia's little Welsh pony leaned drowsily against the board fence beneath a pin oak, and Olivia herself

waited, smiling excitedly. On a tether she was holding a new pony—a skittish chestnut foal with an
unusually blond mane and tail.

"I bought him at the pony auction over at Chincoteague," Olivia's father was saying. "He's wild.
Needs training. But once he's in shape, he'll be a
real gentle ride—for you."

Mary looked at the pony, speechless, as his
words sank in.

"Happy birthday!" Olivia laughed, handing
Mary the tether.

Later, at home, Aunt Lucille raged, "I never gave
that man leave to buy you a pony! And I hope you
don't expect to bring it here to *my* farm. I can
hardly keep us out of the poorhouse now, on a wid-
ow's pension. How am I supposed to feed a horse?
You've got no place putting on airs, like that rich
'horsy' set." She continued muttering and stewing
about the incredible presumption of some folks.

With a dull gray feeling in her heart, Mary politely refused the gift of the pony.

"Why?" Olivia asked as they stood running
their hands along the pony's sleek sides. "He's still
yours. Daddy was planning on keeping him here
anyway—so we can ride together. It doesn't make
any difference, does it?"

Mary fingered the pony's blond forelock, then
drew her hand away. She felt angry at Aunt Lucille.
Also angry, in a confused way, at Olivia's father.
Why give her a gift she could never fully own? Stiffly
she replied, "No, it doesn't make any difference."

In school, Mary had to walk past whispering clots of girls, always with the uncomfortable feeling that they had somehow learned her shameful secret. At the church youth fellowship she sat beside Olivia but always felt the outsider. And so she devoted all the energy in her soul to art class, to mastering color, to blending and perfecting the forms of beauty.

Only the ninth-grade mixer upset the careful borders she built around her private, inner world.

Olivia had talked her into going, and all through the dance Mary felt the boys watching her—and one in particular. Sweating, wearing too-tight neckties, punching each other on the arm, the boys stayed on one side of the gym through most of the evening.

Despite Olivia's intensely dark features and curly black hair and Mary's blond hair and fair complexion, people often mistook them for sisters, perhaps because they were together so much. Olivia's looks and fiery loyalty were so much like the character of Maggie Tulliver in the Victorian novel *The Mill on the Floss* that when they'd discovered the book in lit class this year, Mary had given her friend the nickname "Mags."

"He's looking at me again, Mags," Mary said irritably as they clung together with a few other girls at the edge of the dance floor.

"Not just looking at you," Olivia quailed, squeezing her arm. "He's coming over here!"

The band was striking up a slow dance. And Walker, whose father owned the feed and hardware store, was, indeed, halfway across the floor, passing under the basketball hoop and headed her way. She couldn't avoid him.

Swallowing hard, so that the angle in his throat disappeared several times, he finally asked, "You wanna dance?"

"Sure," she said, flashing a severe look at Olivia, who was bugging her eyes at Mary from behind his back.

In fact, Walker was the one boy Mary did not want to dance with. When she'd seen him at track meets, his T-shirt and gym shorts flapped scarecrow-like about his arms and legs. And he had a space between his front teeth, which gave him the gap-toothed grin he was now flashing at her in relief and gratitude.

There were other boys—handsome, muscled boys—she did like. Their masculine air of nonchalance, their unconcern with girls, their easy power drew her. Yet the moment any one of them showed the slightest interest, she recoiled.

But it was only Walker who'd had enough courage to ask her to dance, despite the hoots and catcalls from the bleachers. And there was something safe and approachable about him.

As they held each other clumsily, Mary could feel his thin shoulder blades through his loose-fitting sportscoat. His hands were hot and moist.

At one moment, as the music was ending—just for a second—he pressed her close. And let her go quickly, too soon to feel her resist.

Amid the scattered applause, he looked at her

with a humble sort of smile and said, "Thank you." And as the band lit into a rock-'n-roll standard, he dared, "Wanna dance again?"

"No," Mary stammered. "Not just now."

When she retreated to her girlfriends, one of them was crowing—"Hoo-*oo*. If you could have seen his eyes! You'd have thought he was driving a Cadillac!" And another winked viciously, "He's got it bad for you, Mary."

Only Olivia detected that something was wrong. She squeezed Mary's arm and quietly asked, "What's the matter?"

With an uncommon coolness, Mary stared at her friend. More than the stolen hug, there was the unexpected joy it brought, fighting against the memory of a dirty, abandoned attic.

"I despise him," she had said coldly, simply. "That's all."

Six

The fog wisps scattered in shreds in the cool-moving air above the stream. She leaned against the oak and squeezed her eyes tightly, as if that could free her of the want that bound her heart.

She'd gotten up from her nest of yellow leaves and followed the stream path down to where the first leather-brown leaves of oak wove into the ragged canopy. She judged herself to be nearing the center part of the forest.

How long had this wilderness surrounded her? How long had the shadows grown and the sun threatened to settle slowly into night? The fairy-tale sense of this forest was waning and the nightmare sense growing, as the light failed and darkness brushed branch and leaf in deeper hues.

A sudden movement in the dimness startled her.

A familiar dark-haired figure in a navy windbreaker was leaning against another tree, so near that in a few steps she would have bumped into him. What disturbed her was the way the stranger just appeared, as if out of nowhere, with the stream's thickening mists curled about him.

He grinned at her in his unreadable way.

"I risked my neck to get to you before he did," he said. "And what did you do? You ignored everything I said. I told you to stay under cover. But no. Here you are, walking along practically in the open. This is the most obvious place for him to find you. Maybe you want to be caught."

She brushed past him angrily, "I don't care to talk to you."

"Come on, Mary," his voice was pleading. "After I tracked you all this way to say how sorry I am for leaving you on your own?"

Over her shoulder she shot back, "You have a weird way of going about it. Besides, you'd be the first man I've ever known who apologized for anything."

So low that she almost didn't hear, he remarked, "What a cold woman."

She wheeled on him. "You have no right to make judgments about me! A man who would leave a woman lost in the woods to save his own skin isn't much of a man. And you don't know anything about me, so keep your opinions to yourself."

Another of those subtle changes collected on his face, the pale, cold eyes turning pained, remorseful.

"I deserved that," he said in a sorry, soulful way.

She told herself she should keep walking. He truly did seem hurt, though. How could men be so selfish one minute, then turn around and be so oversensitive?

"You didn't come all the way back here just to apologize," she said. "So why *did* you come?"

He studied his shoe tops, like a little boy. "You might not like this—but I thought you needed somebody to watch out for you."

"Why wouldn't I like it? Because you think I'm one of those hostile women who hates men?" she said sarcastically. She had a sudden thought that she sounded like Aunt Lucille.

If his intent was to keep her talking, he'd succeeded.

"Come on," he said quietly. "You know I didn't mean that. It's just that a lot of women today hate men who want to take care of them. Sure, I was a little haughty back there. But it's just a defense. I've been kicked in the teeth by more than one woman. You know the type."

So he also had a difficult history. She wondered what had brought him into this bizarre wilderness, what secrets he was running from. "And you think I'm not *that type*," she replied.

"No—you're not cold. You're sensitive to what people feel." He was watching her all the while as if gauging her response. "I saw how you reacted to me a minute ago. So my guess is you're very intelligent. Very intuitive. Not likely to be fooled by anyone. And you do accept my apology, don't you?"

She rolled her eyes. Maybe his overbearing manner was only a defense. "Yeah. Sure. Apology accepted."

With this small victory, his face relaxed into an easier smile, lending a warm charm to his features.

It was getting much colder now, and the wind was picking up. She rubbed her hands to warm them.

"We've got to be moving on," he said.

"Just a minute." She held back. "You still haven't told me your name."

The charming smile spread until he was beaming at her full force. "You're the intuitive one. Why don't you take a guess? Okay, you're rolling your eyes again—but indulge me just this one thing. Take a stab at it. Come on."

It was the kind of foolish gambit women fell for in singles' bars. Yet she let herself study him. This new side—this sensitive vulnerability—had found its mark inside her.

Finally, hardly able to believe she was going along with this silly game, she ventured a guess. "Michael. You look like a Michael."

His eyes widened. "That *is* my name. You're incredible!"

"You're conning me," she replied, but her smile was unreserved. "How do I know I can trust you?"

The soulfulness eased back into his face. "How do you know anything about anyone? You risk. And right now you can't afford not to trust me," he said. "Are you coming?"

She held out a moment longer, but it was a mere formality. If he was keeping something from her— like his real identity, why he was here—could she fault him when she had her own privacies?

Michael, if that was his name, was intriguing. Magnetic. Somehow he'd managed to turn the situation around. She wasn't ready to trust him fully, but she couldn't just stand here. The wind was sharp now, damp and cutting.

"All right," she said confidently, as if it were her idea. "Let's go."

Soon they had covered a good bit of ground, but the air warmed only a little.

That was because Michael insisted they cross over to the right side of the stream and head for better cover in the overgrown part of the forest. Quickly she found herself scratched and irritable—and confused as to direction. At one especially gloomy bend in the path she stumbled and Michael reached out to break her fall. Though her hands were cold, his felt warm.

He was also full of questions—not about her life, but about the moment when she'd first awakened at the waterfall. He made her repeat that part to him, and one detail seemed to fix his attention.

"Like I said, I saw this piercing light," she explained as they walked. "It felt as if my insides were being probed, and I wanted to hide. The core of this light was sparkling with really fiery colors. Then I woke up."

"Was this light anything like what you saw out in the clearing?"

Her jaw dropped. "How did you—? Wait a minute. Did you follow me all the way out to that clearing? Why didn't I hear you?" she demanded.

"When you've been in this place as long as I

have, you learn to move around invisibly, so to speak. Don't you remember anything else about the light?" he persisted. "Think."

"I don't recall. Why is it so important?"

"I'm not sure. It's what I'm trying to find out. I think it has something to do with the reason you were brought here."

Now she ventured a question of her own. "You never told me exactly how you got here—'behind' the world, or wherever we are."

Michael stared at her, as if surprised by the abrupt shift, and as if she'd asked something too personal.

"I don't want you to think I'm putting you off," he finally replied, "but it's best that I don't tell you— in case you're caught. Please trust me. We don't need to know each other's secrets, do we? You've got to protect me, and I'll protect you."

They struggled on through the underbrush, and she wanted to ask him what he thought about the strange freezing wall of wind, or about the hunter's unexplainable retreat when he might have caught her. But deeper fears were triggering in her mind.

"When we were up on the mountain, you told me that this was a place of reckoning, where the deepest things in our hearts could be exposed. Well, I've been wondering about that," she said. "Everyone makes mistakes, right? Even big mistakes. So isn't it enough just to say you're sorry for whatever they think you did wrong?"

"Do you think it's enough to be sorry?" he

countered. "Even assuming that you are sorry, you have to correct what you did wrong. Isn't that what they always told you growing up?"

"What if the thing you've done can never be corrected?" she finally posed, uncomfortably.

"Then someone has to pay," he replied summarily. "That's the way it is, isn't it?"

She fell silent. Perhaps he would think it was just the sudden rise of harsh wind that brought the tears to her eyes. A weight was trying to settle on her, to crush the life out of her spirit. Other people had always made choices for her—choices that wounded her. Was it fair—when she'd made one choice, all on her own—that she should bear such a weight of guilt? She was glad he didn't ask her any more questions.

The wind had been catching up with them since Michael had struck a path away from the stream, perpendicular to it, apparently making for an escape route he knew. The frosty gusts mounted, slapping blown leaves in their faces.

A little more rough going and they came out of the oak trees into a small clearing on the edge of a cliff. The sheer drop before them was high enough so they could see over the tops of the trees below.

They'd traveled so far into the natural amphitheater of the forest that she could no longer see any open land. She thought they were more than halfway through the forest now, but halfway to what?

The blue-red sky she'd noticed from the mountainside appeared even thicker now, as if a literal screen or veil were drawn across the horizon. Briefly, she wondered why she could see nothing in the distance behind this odd, concealing sky.

"How do we get down from here?" she asked, cautiously glancing over the edge. Wind-driven leaves spiraled down the dangerous spill of stone. The icy wall would capture them for sure if they didn't hurry.

"There's only one way."

Michael led her to one side of the ledge where several huge boulders rested against one another. Pointing to a narrow opening between the rocks, he explained, "We go down through here. There's a passage."

"You didn't tell me about this," she resisted, her fear of dark, shut-in places roaring within her. But by now she had to raise her voice above the pitch and moan of the wind. "Why can't we just find a way to climb down?"

"You've got to trust me in this!" he shouted back. "There's no other way."

Surely this wasn't the only way down. But in the fearful pressure of the moment, she was confused and panicked. In any case, Michael was not waiting for her approval. He lowered himself inside the rocky opening with a brief "Come on."

Obediently she followed.

Inside the passage, the air was a little warmer, though it came in a damp draft. Relief from the wind made up a little for the low ceiling and the clammy closeness of the walls. And the floor, which sloped in a gradual decline, was mostly sand spread over solid rock, not muddy as she'd imagined a cave might be. Somewhere up ahead, thankfully, an open shaft let in a filtering of light, so her eyes adjusted quickly to the near-dark.

Ahead of her, Michael was moving in a crouch, his knuckles nearly touching the floor. "This way," he directed, his voice coming back as a muffled echo. "Stay close. We don't want to get separated. It's tricky. You'll never get out on your own."

Hunching down, she shouldered her way through the tunnel after him. "Slow down a little." She scrambled to keep up with the form vanishing into shadow up ahead in the turning passage.

The ceiling rose a little, but never enough to allow them to stand upright. Fortunately, the weak light persisted. From somewhere came the echoing drip of water on stone.

Eventually they came to a place where the tunnel forked. The opening to the right was extremely narrow but taller, and it was lit with a pale light from some opening above. Her heart sank when Michael nodded toward the other passage, which was hardly more than a crawl space, and pitch-black.

Seizing him by one shoulder, she held him from plunging in ahead of her. When he turned, his breath came in cool drafts against her face. The darkness erased his features, except for a pale flicker of emotion in his eyes. "If we get separated, don't worry. I'll come for you."

"I can't go in there," she confessed.

"You have to."

"I can't."

"It's impossible to go back now."

She fought the sick feeling in her throat. From outside and above, the echo of moaning wind grew louder.

She stared into the winter-pale eyes, refusing to dissolve into a hysterical female. The way out couldn't be much farther—the cliff was not that high. She steadied herself and took a deep breath. "Okay."

Lowering himself onto his stomach, Michael pushed forward, disappearing into the opening.

On her stomach in sand, she slid inside after him. The blackness was staggering. Inadvertently, Michael kicked some sand in her face. She held back, but only a little for fear of losing contact.

Twice her head glanced off a down-jut in the roof, which knocked showers of loose dirt onto her hair and neck.

Hugging the sandy floor closer, she forced herself not to think *up*. Hardly able to believe she'd let him talk her into this, she called, "Are we almost out?"

His reply was muffled by the close black air.

Suddenly her cheek bumped up against the sole of his shoe. He had stopped crawling and must have turned his face back toward her, because she heard him say clearly, "Here it is. This way. Quick."

Apparently they'd come to another fork.

There was a scuffling of sand in her face, and he was moving on, angling to the left again. She let him get a head start to avoid having more sand kicked in her face.

Now the passage pressed so low that her ribs barely slid through the opening. The darkness was weighty, disorienting. She was starting to feel dizzy and had to concentrate to keep moving. Only by slithering could she pull her way along, excruciatingly slow. Perspiration beaded and chilled on her temples. The air was stagnant with mold.

In the complete blackness, she sensed herself crawling past several side passages—felt them gaping open like the mouths of dead men. Were they ten yards into this detestable crack, or twenty? From the tightness of rock all around, her own breathing echoed in her ears, close and labored. Still she kept crawling, seeking a final turn and the open air. And then, with one small push, her ribs were seized entirely between rock.

How could he have made it through here? She frantically struggled, trying to get through. *Or maybe . . .* Every muscle froze: He was no longer ahead of her. How had she missed the turn-off?

She listened for the rustle of movement.

Nothing but silence and cold stone. Rock gripped her ribs in a vise.

She was caught at a slightly head-down angle. From above, her back was being pressed by mighty tons of rock, waiting to crush her.

"Mi—chael," she breathed, unable to expel much air.

There was no sound. Nothing from behind or ahead. She was captured and alone in the blackness.

His warning came to her—*"You'll never get out*

on your own"—and the seed of fear burst its shell.

Instantly, everything inside her wanted to push back against the heavy, heavy weight that pinned her, as if she could force the rock to budge. *I need air.* It took every bit of mental strength to seize control of herself, body and soul, and fight that futile urge, which she dimly recognized as panic. Panic would be certain death.

The pressure from her downward angle was building in her head. She commanded her breathing to slow and her mind to go blank. She remembered reading somewhere that in moments of crisis people receive flashes of instinct that tell them what to do. This was her hope.

She waited, breathing shallow. Nothing came.

She held on longer, grappling with the urge to struggle. To scream. The monolith wanted to push down on her. *Why did I ever let Michael bring me in here? Why didn't I follow my own instincts earlier and find a way to climb down?*

In the cold darkness, her head pounding, she began to imagine pulsing light. Ahead. So strong. And in the silence, a word trying to pierce through.

I'm blacking out, she thought. Her face tingled. Lights burst in her head.

Like a whisper inside, the word came again . . .
seek . . .

Impossible. She couldn't press her ribs forward through the rocks if she wanted to. And even if she could, it might wedge her more.

But what if. . . ?

. . . in the dark heart. . . .

She called on her last reserve of strength and, against all good sense, pressed forward into the crack.

Only to trap herself tighter.

You idiot. You're making it worse. Give up.

But a courage seemed to come from outside her. A calmness. And again she dug her toes in the dirt, forcing her way.

This time, to her shock and relief, her ribs actually slid through the stone vise, and she dragged her lower body through with no trouble. Lying in sand, in a small hollow of the rock, she went limp and let her head clear.

There was no light ahead, only more darkness. No matter. A sense told her she was going to make it after all.

With a few more lurches forward, she found that the ceiling was lifting above her and the floor was less sloping. She no longer had to pull along on her elbows, and could soon crawl on all fours.

Hints of light and fresh air lured her on. The ceiling kept rounding upward until finally she was able to struggle to her feet in a bell-shaped passage. Stumbling, she made it through the last brightening descent into the open.

Out in the free air, she drew deep satisfying breaths as her mind calmed and her legs stopped shaking. *I never thought I'd be so glad to see this forest again.* She drew another deep breath, savoring the earthy freshness, feeling stronger. To her amazement, for the first time in a long while she actually felt the will to live.

This was no place to stop, though. Nor the time to wonder over the strong influences that had fought within her in the darkness. One had nearly caused her to give in to the weight of despair—the other had given her courage.

The wind had reached the cliff above while she'd been inside the passage. She could see the glacial wall moving forward faster than when she'd first encountered it above the waterfall, its front edge ivying down the rocks in tendrils of killing frost. She could see one perfect autumn leaf frozen in midair, as if suspended in crystal.

Only now did she remember that Michael promised to find her if they were separated in the cave. There was one other small opening leading out from the rock face. Thinking he might still be inside looking for her, she leaned inside and called.

No response.

He wouldn't have left me—not after following me all the way through the woods to help me. He said he'd protect me, she reminded herself. Maybe he thought she'd escaped already and gone on into the woods ahead of him. *He's probably up ahead looking for me.*

Behind her, the world was rapidly dying in ice, sealing over the stones that had nearly been her tomb.

Seven

Michael now seemed to be her only hope, and she fled after him through the trees, eager to catch up. But below the cliff and the cave, the forest was even more confusing to her than it had been before.

The light was much weaker now, like the small slice of time just after sunset, when the trees are losing their solid shape. Also, the ordeal in the cave had disrupted all sense of bearing. She knew she must be headed into the farther edge of the forest, but she had no idea where the stream was.

The forest gradually gave way to a maze of boulders, some towering half as high as the trees, like the walls of a massive labyrinth. She stared at them for some time in consternation, but one thing she was sure of: She could not go back into those murky depths behind her.

Entering between the first of the giant stones, she completely lost her already-failing sense of direction. With it went the hope and confidence she'd gained from surviving the cave.

I wish I could get back to the stream, she thought wistfully, missing its unusual water lights and comforting voice. Then almost at once, she found herself emerging from the maze at last, where she encountered another dense wall of trees. Mercifully, there was much less thorn here and only a few mottled-green mounds of rhododendron.

Which way now?

The air only hinted of the oncoming iciness, but it was cool enough that a few faint, lonely wisps of mist drifted along the floor of shed leaves. She wondered hopefully if that meant the stream was not too far away.

A momentary movement in the distance, down where a grove of pine trees disappeared into the rising mists, made her wonder if it was Michael, searching for her.

She almost called out, then checked herself, remembering the hunter. Most likely he was still over on the far side of the forest, since he'd left the clearing headed in the opposite direction. Michael had been sure the man would never look for her on this side of the stream. On the other hand, why risk it?

Cautiously, quietly, she picked her way down through the trees and moving fog toward the pine grove. A little farther, the mists rose to her knees.

Then, in the unexpected way it has, the fog swirled up around her. Instantly she was forced to feel her way along, groping from tree to tree. The fog thickened, surrounding her, closing her within a damp prison of sightlessness. She drew up her collar but could not keep out the dismal isolation of it.

"I'm so sick of being alone," she muttered suddenly, as her hands felt for the next tree. "All my life I've been alone, and I *hate* it."

At the back of her mind, someone answered her: *You'll always be alone. No one cares about you.*

A determined voice countered the words of despair: *You can't give up now.* Two forces wrestling again. She recognized another familiar feeling: a sense that larger forces always seemed to manipulate her life, powering her in directions she didn't want to go.

The mist dewed her hair and moistened her cheeks. She sank down at the base of a tree and leaned her head back against it, hoping the fog might pass. . . .

. . ."Art school is out of the question," Aunt Lucille said. "You're not wasting *my* money on that."

Actually, it was not Aunt Lucille's money but a trust fund Oliver had willed to Mary. It became available when she turned eighteen and would pay for at least part of her college education. The rest she would cover with a student loan. Unfortunately, Aunt Lucille was the controlling trustee of the fund.

At seventy-nine, the salt and vinegar in Aunt Lucille's personality had watered down a bit. "I do want you to get a good education," she insisted.

That sounded kind, but Mary decided that the real reason Aunt Lucille refused to let her go to art school, which was close to home, was that she'd rather Mary was *away* at college.

Aunt Lucille chose a small, select women's college in the Virginia Blue Ridge where "good families" sent their young daughters—or at least that's where a number of wild and strong-willed girls of wealth were packed off to, in hopes that someone there could hammer them into some semblance of a lady. Aunt Lucille had her way, of course, and Mary's only resort was to concentrate on the fine arts and *think* of it as art school.

Upon her arrival, Mary discovered that, even in these days, *de rigueur* dress for a campus ball included cashmere sweater sets, pearls and certain expensive colognes.

"A lady," explained the residence matron during orientation week, "is provocative, but sophisticated."

And one of the girls said, under her breath, "She means, only go home with a man who has money."

Even if it was a relief to be away from Aunt Lucille, Mary felt uncomfortable with these girls and very much out of her league. She knew of no one else here who had a student loan. Only Olivia's frequent letters—with reports about her new decorating business, about her boyfriend Harlan, and about the church youth fellowship she was leading—gave Mary any sense of belonging somewhere.

She certainly didn't belong at this school. And despite the courses mapped out for her, she felt isolated, directionless. . . .

. . . While she sat there, shivering and alone, the unearthly fog parted. A small spark winked at her from down in the vanishing grove of pine trees, so faint she thought it was only her imagination. The mists drifted back across, then parted again, revealing a steady glow—a pale, luminous roundness, moving into the depths of fog and forest.

Something told her this was Michael. *He's made a torch, and he's looking for me,* she surmised. *He'll never see me through this pea soup.*

Quickly she began feeling her way downhill toward the grove, twice scratching her cheek against low limbs.

It was the fragrance of fir and the soft brush of long needles against her face that told her she'd arrived at the grove. Ahead, deep among the pines, the light was searching about slowly. Still wary, she called in a stage whisper, "Michael!"

No reply.

The light moved on ahead. Then vanished in another rolling tide of fog.

When it reappeared, it had stopped, as if waiting. Hovering above the ground, it lit up a small circle of bristled branches and cones. Then it moved on.

Huge, rough trunks, sticky with pine pitch, marked her way. The pulse was racing in her neck. The pale light was pulsing, too. Just slightly. Pulsing with her pulse, it seemed. Guiding her.

And then, reaching out in the fog for something solid, steady, her hand met with nothing. She reeled forward on uneven ground, fighting for balance.

The light stopped, only yards ahead. She could sense a presence.

"Michael?" she whispered, stumbling forward.

Pale and beckoning, the light floated in the mists. She could reach him. In just a few more steps . . .

A peal of thunder broke suddenly—and a second light flashed through the fog, instantly dazzling the woods a brilliant white and overpowering the paler one. In that illuminated second, she saw two things: She was standing by a great pine tree that was twisted and scarred as if by lightning— and out of that second light a man was coming toward her through the fog.

His voice she knew instantly.

"You thought you were running away from danger, didn't you, Mary? But instead you ran straight for it. I'm here to help you. Come with me. Now!" said the hunter in his low, commanding way.

She was like some small creature, paralyzed by the presence of a larger being. Again that quiet voice inside urged that she give herself up.

"No, Mary!" shouted another voice from behind her—it was Michael's. "Don't go to him. Take my hand!"

She wheeled, seeing nothing in the confusion of light and mist and darkness.

Like smoke out of the smoke, Michael flew at her from behind, his hand reaching. Only for a split second did she hesitate, then thrust her hand in his.

Pulling her after him, Michael plunged them back into the concealing mists. How could he see at all in this confounding fog? Yet he dodged them around wind-fallen trees and patches of under-growth without a pause.

From behind, the figure that loomed in the light, not moving, called out, "You think you can win, but there's no point in running. Let her come to me!"

Michael's hand squeezed tighter around hers, and they continued running until they were out of the pine grove and some distance into the forest. Suddenly Michael dropped to his knees behind a rotting stump, pulling her down with him.

When his breathing slowed a little, he said, "I never thought he'd come in here after you. He wants you in the worst way."

Behind, there was not even a trace of the brilliant light.

"He never . . . chased us," she replied, still gasping. "Strange . . . don't you think? When he almost had us both?"

Michael did not answer, but kept looking back. She could feel his warmth from running. Gradually, her own breathing slowed. She bit her lip. "I have to ask—please don't be upset with me, Michael—but it's about back there. In the passage. Didn't you know I'd fallen behind you?"

He turned and fixed her with an offended look. "Know? Of course I knew. But not until it was too late. I was so intent on getting us out of there—because I knew how panicky you were—that I sacrificed my own safety for you. I was almost killed, Mary.

"Once I realized you'd taken a wrong turn behind me I was worried sick. I went back to look for you, and got lost crawling through all those turns. I managed to get out before the ice sealed off the cave. I hoped like crazy that somehow you'd gotten out another way and had run on ahead of me to wait.

"Then I got lost in this fog—until I spotted you walking into his trap back there."

He paused. "You did know it was a trap, didn't you? I mean, you weren't trying to lose me in the cave, were you?"

She felt both incensed and guilty—and the twist of suspicion in his voice rankled.

"You can't really believe I'm on his side!" she countered. "Didn't you hear what he said to me? I know it was a trap!" She blew out a long, exasperated breath. "I'm just going to ignore all these questions, Michael."

His expression eased into a stiff smile, which she took to mean that she'd regained a measure of his goodwill. But if it was not Michael she'd seen searching with a torch, then what was the pale light she'd been following?

At the moment, however, another question was more urgent. Did he have any idea how they were going to escape from this forsaken place? Was there a way out—or was running useless? She was about to ask him, but Michael swiftly raised one finger to his lips.

"We can't stay here," he whispered. "He'll be coming for us—if he isn't already. I've got to do something."

"What?"

"Lead him on a wild-goose chase."

"What about me?" she countered. "What am I supposed to do?"

Michael tenderly slipped one arm around her shoulders. "Give me some time to lead him away from here," he instructed. "After that, start heading downhill again. When you get past the grove, bear to the right—away from the stream. There's a passageway I've been trying to lead you to all along."

This was good news—finally. "A way out of this place?"

"If I can just keep you away from him long enough," he replied, "we can beat him at his own game."

She gripped his arm, still unnerved. "Don't go. Please," she begged. "What if you don't come back? You're my only hope of getting out of here."

His eyes met hers fully, with an inscrutable look that was closest, perhaps, to satisfaction. He whispered, "Is that the only reason you want me to come back?"

Before she could answer, he was up and moving away into the deeper darkness. "I promise I'll be back. I can outsmart him. But you start heading for the passageway, not the stream. Remember that. Don't wait for me. And don't worry—I'll always find you somehow. I have so far, haven't I?"

When he was out of sight, lost in the fog, she

continued to stare after him for a long time.

Curiously, the pale light she'd followed into the grove—or at least one very much like it—appeared again. So did a second, greater light, and by comparison the lesser one looked weak and ghostly, like foxfire from some haunted forest hollow. The two lights drifted, then seemed to lock in on each other and draw close. They paused at some distance from her, like combatants in a tournament.

All at once, both began to pulse and flare, like cannon shots of split lightning; and terrifying rumbles of thunder rolled, muffled through the fog.

So it continued, volley upon volley, this argument of lights.

Where was Michael? And what was it about him—about most men she'd ever met—that was so confusing to her? Why did men get you to trust them, then hurt you—or just leave?

She watched in wonder as more flashes pierced the fog. Mesmerizing clouds and illuminations overwhelming her. . . .

———

. . . At the fall semester's opening gala, she met Cam. He was a second-semester senior at their "brother" college eight miles away, and she was a sophomore.

Mary's roommate, ever in the know, elbowed her. "International business major. Captain of the tennis team," she grinned conspiringly. "His father has a seat on the stock exchange. They've got *big* bucks."

It wasn't the money that attracted her, though, or even that he was athletic and darkly handsome. Mary was taken by the way Cam stepped so boldly into her long isolation and ended it overnight with lavish attention. He awakened her to unheard-of possibilities—with surprise picnics, cello concerts, roses and a card delivered late at night, the gift of an ornate Austrian music box. It was as if he were peeling back a bristly rind to reveal for her the tender and sweet fruit of life.

On a Friday in early October, Mary accepted his invitation to spend a weekend with his parents at their hunting lodge in the Blue Ridge. "They'd love to have you join us. And so would I."

Mary was delighted. It sounded so normal, so accepting of her.

As his sports car negotiated the mountain curves, Cam kept touching her hand gently whenever he wanted to make a point in conversation, or when she made him laugh.

"What do you like to do?" he asked at one point.

"Well, summers I help with the youth fellowship at my home church. My friend, Olivia, leads it. I like canoeing with the kids and—" She broke off mid-sentence, because Cam was chuckling.

"What is it?"

Fighting back an amused grin, he said, "I didn't mean what do you do as charity work. I meant, what do you like to do for fun? Sailing? Tennis? Horses? Travel? You've got to be from old Virginia money to be at this college, but you're so secretive about yourself. Nobody seems to know much about you. So what's your family into?"

She dodged his probing because she was uncomfortable with the truth. His world and hers were too far apart. She couldn't tell him about Aunt Lucille, or that she'd tried to contact her mother once, two years ago, only to be told: "I've got a new life out here in California, and it would be very inconvenient for me to see you right now." So she skipped back to her first reply.

"I like working with the youth fellowship. It's important to me. I grew up with it. And I guess it makes me feel connected to something outside myself. You don't find that funny, I hope."

Cam sobered. "I wasn't making fun of you. Honestly. If church is something you need, I think that's great. Spirituality is great—for some people. But for me, real life is out there in the big world, where you can make things happen. But look, let's forget this and have a good time. Okay?"

Mary let it slide. After all, they didn't have to match in everything. And Cam could be so charming and thoughtful—like the huge bouquet of roses he'd sent the time she passed a horrendous math exam.

When they drove in, his parents had not yet arrived at the lodge. An Indian summer warmth invited them outside for a soft afternoon, arm in arm along an old bridle path. By early evening, as Cam lit a fire on the stone hearth, they were still alone.

"Some snag with an international bank, no doubt," he offered in explanation of his parents' delay. From a mahogany cabinet he pulled out a crystal decanter and two snifters, and began pouring.

"I'm used to Mother and Dad not showing up on cue," he said casually. "I suppose you had a more or less regular family life. Would you like a brandy?"

Mary politely declined and, once again, ducked the reference to her family. "We'd better go. I don't think we should stay. Not if there's a chance they won't show."

He shrugged. "My guess is they'll be in by midnight. That's not unlike them either. Why ruin a good weekend? It could be fun." He added, obliquely, "We are adults."

It was an unwise decision, she knew that. Perhaps it was because she didn't want Cam to think she was an unsophisticated "country girl," or because she wanted to believe him, but she decided to spend the night—alone in the guest room.

In the morning, when Cam's parents were still nowhere to be seen, she suspected the truth. And then he came downstairs, still in his robe.

"We've got to go back," Mary said, turning away when he tried to slip his arms around her. "It's not right for me to stay any longer."

Yawning, he stretched with the languid energy of a young lion. Again he reached for her. "What I'm feeling for you at this moment is what's right."

"I want to leave," she insisted. "Now."

On the drive back, Cam was repentant. "You probably think I engineered things this way . . ." He let the idea hang in the air.

"The thought crossed my mind," Mary said.

"Even if I did, you can't blame me for the way you make me feel. I can't figure out why some other guy hasn't put a diamond on your finger."

That softened her. She smiled. "You must think I'm a sucker for a good line."

Seeing her relax, he smiled, too. When he touched her cheek, she did not pull away. "If it is a line, you don't think I'd admit it, do you?"

From then on, it was taken for granted they would see each other in most of their free time. He barraged her with small gifts of jewelry, flowers, perfume, evenings at a local dinner theater. And if he suddenly, without a word, stood her up for a weekend date, he covered with candy or a book of poetry, but no explanation. "It's personal business" was all he'd tell her. "Family, you might say."

She had not yet met Cam's parents. Something always seemed to prevent it at the last minute. And if Cam seemed totally uninterested in her art, her bike club trips, or her involvement with the church group at home—well, Mary mentally erased these awkward shadows from the happy portrait she envisioned, of a young couple with an exciting life ahead.

Then, as Cam's January graduation approached, he began to say *we* when he spoke of the future.

Put simply, Mary thought she was falling in love

for the first time. She just knew, in her heart, a proposal was coming. ("What's he waiting for?" her roommate complained.)

After his departure to New York in January, where he went to work at his father's investment firm, there were long-distance phone calls. They came less frequently, though, as his job demanded additional time. Mary began occupying herself more and more with her artwork. Color-splashed paintings filled the walls of her room.

In the spring a call from Cam set her nerves jangling. "This is important, Mary," he said. "I need to see you."

Two days later Cam's new silver Mercedes eased up to the curb outside her residence hall. When he stepped out, Mary rushed to put her arms around him, but he kept the opened car door braced between them.

"Before we talk," he said nervously, "there's someone you have to meet."

Mary hadn't noticed through the car's dark-tinted glass that he'd brought someone with him. A gorgeous brunette, who looked as if she owned stock in Saks Fifth Avenue, slid out from the passenger side.

"This is Christina," Cam offered, trying to control his flush of embarrassment. "My fiancee."

When Cam angled a moment alone, Mary was beyond furious. "What kind of game have you been playing with me?"

"I never made any promises."

"No—you never did, did you? Then how could

you do this to *her*? Where were you hiding her all this time?"

"She wanted to live in Europe for a while. She knew we'd be stuck in New York after the wedding. I was lonely. You seemed lonely, too."

"What about all your big 'plans' for *our* future?"

"I got a little carried away. And I knew it was what you wanted to hear. That was wrong," he said seriously. As an effort to shoulder blame, it was unconvincing. "But, Mary, I thought you could see all along that it was impossible for us to be serious. You knew my family had big plans for me. And your family . . ." He faltered.

"What do you know about my family?"

"I've asked around. What does it matter?"

Mary was stunned. "Why did you keep asking me about my family if you knew I wasn't 'your type'?"

"You didn't seem to want to admit it. I just thought it would be better for you if you did. I accepted you for what you are."

"For what I am?" she repeated bitterly. "Well, thank you so much, Mr. Friend-to-the-lowly-orphan. Maybe you can write off all those gifts on your income tax as a charitable donation.

"And here's a little charity for you," she flung at him. "I'm not going to tell the lovely, talented and rich Christina about the weekend at 'Daddy's lodge' and how 'serious' you wanted to be then—or tell her about the phone calls and the gifts."

Cam stared at the sidewalk between his shoes. "You're a good person, Mary. Sorry isn't the right thing to say for what I've done to you, is it?" This was remorseless, really—little more than a buy-off. But Mary had already turned her back on him, the mists of humiliation clouding her eyes.

"For what you've done," she said, "sorry doesn't even come close."

Eight

The unearthly lights had given up their conflict, but Michael had not returned.

And apparently the ice wall had not drawn near enough to cool and settle the fog, for thick mists, like unseen hands, continued to brush across her face. She drew up her knees and hugged them tightly in the gray darkness, listening blindly for the faintest noise.

The hunter could sneak up on me and I'd never hear him until it was too late. Immediately, she was sorry for allowing the unsettling thought.

Michael had told her to give him a little time before setting out. *But there is no real sense of time in here,* she thought. He might have been gone ten minutes, or two hours.

She'd rested at several spots, but never really slept, even though it seemed that days had passed since she'd been in here. And the deeper she'd come into this forest, the more this too-long-awake, too-wary feeling had worked into a deep soul weariness.

At once it occurred to her that this feeling had tormented her most of her life: Ever since she was a girl, she'd suffered under an always-alert, acute self-consciousness. It never left her alone, this hellish wakefulness—this fear that if she let down her guard even for a moment something painful and terrible would happen.

What a morbid frame of mind you've fallen into, she told herself, shaking off these ideas.

Quietly she got up and began to feel her way along between the damp, close, silent trees, finding her direction only by the downward slope of the ground. Was the hunter hiding behind one of those rough trunks?

Her passing stirred ghostly risings in the fog. Almost-figures, which lifted and swirled away in small eddies. They were trying to remind her—she knew it now—of all that she did not want to remember.

She blinked them away, these troubled scatterings of her past. What was it in the nature of this place that kept drawing out hidden depths of memory? It was as if she were being pushed or drawn inexorably—to where? To what moment in time?

A worm-knot of sick fear turned in the pit of her stomach. She had to stop and lean her forehead against a tree, her vision beginning to swim again. Why would the confusion of her past not leave her alone? What good did it do to recall those things now?

And still the figures rose, refusing to stay buried . . .

—————

. . . The summer after Mary's graduation from college, only a month after she'd taken a job at a Washington ad agency, Aunt Lucille died. She'd had a fall in the late spring, a broken hip that never healed, followed by pneumonia, and then a peaceful death one sultry August night. Sad, because for some unexplained reason the old woman had mellowed a good bit.

In her last letter to Mary, she had written cryptically, "We must talk." They never had the chance, and Mary saw this as yet another "unlucky deal of the cards."

Immediately, the farm was sold by Lucille's side of the family. Without any note or letter, Uncle Wallace, the estate's executor, sent Mary a check for a thousand dollars.

All this left Mary with a sense that beneath the ground of her life, a main root had been abruptly severed. She had not expected to feel that. Days melted one into the next, directionless. Olivia was her only connection to anything like a family or a home back in Walnut Level.

Now, on Fridays, when Mary beat the afternoon traffic out of the city and drove down the eastern shore, she was drawn by that single, anchoring friendship.

On one of those Friday evenings, she allowed herself to be corralled by Olivia into decorating the high school gymnasium for a class reunion. The familiar smell of paste wax met her as she walked, crepe paper and tape in hand, into the empty gym.

"Am I it—the whole decoration committee?" she asked, turning on Olivia.

"Of course not," her friend replied spiritedly. "I rounded up one other volunteer."

Mary did not at first recognize the man who, ten minutes later, came quietly into the gym, carrying a ladder. He was tall and well-built, sandy-haired, with a gentle down-home bearing. Relieving himself of the ladder he extended his hand, and gave her a soft smile. "Remember me? Walker?"

The transformation was astounding. The gangly, gap-toothed boy had matured into this quietly confident, attractive man.

"Can you believe it?" he offered, by way of explaining himself. "I got into the service. ROTC. Actually made it into officer training. I was going to make the military my career, but my dad passed away last year. Left me the feed and hardware store. So—here I am, back in Walnut Level."

There was something about Walker that, as the evening went on and they worked side by side, made her increasingly uneasy. She couldn't put her finger on it. When she talked—about Washington, her hopes of succeeding with her painting someday—he listened intently, genuinely. But he offered little about himself. Accustomed as Mary was to the braggadocio of the men who pursued her, his reserve made her uncomfortable. Mary knew it was perverse to be irritated by a man whose quiet, unassuming nature drew her out and succeeded in making her comfortable, but she couldn't help it.

By the end of the evening she only wanted to escape him.

"You manufactured that little decorations committee, didn't you?" Mary challenged Olivia the next morning.

They were seated at Olivia's kitchen table, sorting through swatches of chintz for one of her especially choosey and irritable customers.

Olivia did not pick up the lead. Instead, she said, "Here I am in the decorating business, when you're the one with the eye for color and beauty. It's not fair."

Mary smiled, recognizing the dodge. "I'll tell you what's not fair, Mags. Everything turns out wonderful for you. I just keep waiting for life to happen for me. You have Harlan. After him, I think all the decent males have been dying at birth."

"There's Walker," Olivia replied, sounding very much like someone who's trying hard not to manipulate. "Since he came back to run the business, he's been asking about you."

It was out of character for Olivia to meddle, and Mary was slightly annoyed. "If there's such a thing as 'Mr. Right,'" she said distantly, "I'll know him when I see him. And believe me, he won't be driving a jacked-up pickup truck with a gun rack in the back window."

Olivia stopped sorting, looking Mary square in face. "That's pretty unkind. Besides, Walker doesn't drive a pickup. Okay, so he's not ivy league, like some of the men you've dated. But he's kind. Good-looking. He's been coming to church lately, and the women nearly fall over dead when he smiles. And he knows about things—like *art*—which you'd discover if you'd give him half a chance. You know, Mary, ever since Cam, you've been really cynical."

That was Olivia—unsparing in love, and unsparing in honesty.

"It's not just Cam," Mary said, irritated. "I've dated a few men since him. And they're all interested in the same things—themselves, sports, politics, money, and guess-what-else. Did I forget to tell you? The last one had a wife and two kids at home. When I found out, he said it was my fault for encouraging him."

"Maybe if you tried meeting a man in church," Olivia offered.

"Where do you think I met that one?"

"Still, it doesn't mean every man in this world is out to hurt you," Olivia challenged. "I could understand when you used to be shy with the boys in school. But I don't understand where this suspicion—this hostile attitude comes from."

Mary never had told Olivia about Uncle Wallace, possibly because she herself spent so much energy not thinking about him. She'd developed a way of handling unpleasant things, like the past, blunting hurts and lies the way an oyster buries a hard grain, entombing them in a smooth milk-coating of non-thought.

"In other words," Mary replied, "just let go of the past. Right?"

Olivia took the opening. "That's not exactly

what I mean, but I'm not sure how to say it. You've had a string of bad ones, that's for sure. It's more that I'm concerned because of what I see happening inside you." Olivia reached across the table and touched Mary's hand. "When we used to play fairy tales, you were always the romantic princess. You used to write poems. I'd like to see that old Mary once in a while."

"I could sing you a round of 'Some Day My Prince Will Come.' "

"That's what I mean. It hurts me to see you becoming so sarcastic."

"Maybe I'm just waking up."

"More like closing off," Olivia said tersely. "So many times I've watched you just turn off your emotions at will. You become almost—almost inhuman, and it's scary."

An uncomfortable silence followed.

After a bit, Mary offered a peace gesture. "I wish I could be like you, Mags. You throw yourself into life. You're so carefree. I enjoy watching what you do for Harlan. He lights up when you're around. And the kids in your youth group, too. So many of them love God because of you. You're a gift to people. You—yourself. And good things just come your way."

Olivia protested, but Mary stopped her. "I know you're going to say, 'It's not me. It's the Lord.' But I pray sometimes, too. And whoever's supposed to be listening hides from me. I feel so lost. As if I'm going nowhere."

Olivia countered. "You're saying that I'm

blessed, and you're not. But you're the one who went to a prestigious college—even if you didn't like it. And you've landed a great job with a top ad agency when there were eleven other applicants. Doesn't that tell you Someone has a hand on your life?"

Mary shrugged at that. "Sketching ads for the *Post* and designing covers for department store catalogs—that's a far cry from having your own gallery. Or even just a showing."

Olivia pushed aside the stack of fabrics and looked at Mary directly. Mary thought she was going to say, "You will someday."

Instead, she said, "Remember when Daddy bought that Chincoteague pony and said it could be yours?"

"Yes."

"I've thought back on that so many times. You never really accepted that pony as your own, did you?"

"Your father boarded it at *your* farm. *He* paid the vet bills. *You* fed it when I couldn't come over."

"You know that was only because your aunt said it was too much trouble to keep a pony at her place," Olivia went on. "But the pony was still yours, even if you couldn't keep it at home. But because you couldn't have it in exactly the way you wanted it, you never accepted it as your own."

"I see what you're getting at," Mary replied. "But can you blame me for wanting to own something—to know that it's all mine and nobody else's? After losing my mother—and Oliver—what do you expect? I wish I didn't feel as if I needed just one special person—who was everything I've ever wanted. But I do," she said.

Both were quiet for a moment, the cloth swatches now forgotten. Then Mary continued. "There's another thing that troubles me. Maybe it's not related. Or maybe it is.

"It's like you have some invisible quality I don't have, Mags. That gift I was talking about—it's inside you. It's all over you. And I wish they sold it in a spray bottle. It's more than just your faith—it's a certain presence that isn't there for me. I believe what you believe. But it doesn't work the same for me.

"It's as if you were chosen and I wasn't. I want to be loved, too. But my life messes up. Living hurts. Inside me, there's just confusion. I believe in God, like you do. I've read the Bible, and I think a lot about things your dad taught us in Sunday school. And I wish that what I believe could change the way I feel and the way I live. But for me it's like some connection is broken."

Olivia said—with such gentleness that Mary could not be offended—"I don't think we really do believe the same things, Mary. At least we don't believe them in the same way yet. But I do know this: God loves you. He longs for you to trust him. He loves you." Her hand was on Mary's again.

She went on. "No matter what it takes, I know he'll prove himself—because he wants to get through to you and show you his love isn't superficial, not like these bozos you've been meeting. He wants you to open up to him at the deepest place inside. But that may cause even more pain, especially if you try to keep out the very people who want to love you."

For no reason she could explain, Mary became suddenly uncomfortable, and wanted to end this conversation.

"I'll take your word for it," she said. "Whenever God's ready, I'm ready. He can find me—if he really wants to."

———

The cherry trees along the mall in front of the Smithsonian museums had blossomed in an early-spring stretch of warm sunny days, then lost all loveliness almost overnight in a hammering wind. As Mary walked beneath them, the trees looked as ragged and stark as the homeless men asleep on the subway gratings.

Today Mary needed to lose herself in the art galleries.

Her spirits had climbed a little with the warm days, but slid into depression with the return of gray, colorless weather. Throughout the fall and winter, after the farm was sold, she'd gone through upheaval—climbing slopes up into moments of a vague, bright joy, only to plunge down the other side into a lost and wandering state of spirit.

One brief sunlit peak came at Valentine's Day, when Olivia and Harlan announced their engagement. But that had ended when a gray voice inside told her this was only a substitute joy. *Why is it that someone as good as Harlan never comes along for you?*

So Olivia's happiness turned into an occasion for envy, then guilt, then a final tipping downhill again into depression. Once, like fingers nervously touching gunmetal, her thoughts even turned to suicide.

When she could squeeze in a long lunch, like today, a trip to the Smithsonian galleries relieved the further numbing effect of endless commercial layouts.

Leaving the ragged cherry trees, Mary walked up the broad granite steps to the National Gallery. Inside the lobby, a harassed-looking grade-school teacher and a blue-suited tour guide were trying to organize and contain an earthquake of second graders. Mary skirted the commotion and headed upstairs to the vast, quiet halls. Only one or two other browsers were ambling along the marble floor.

She had some favorite pieces here. For a few days she'd been thinking about one of them in particular, a portrait, and now she stopped in front of it, staring silently.

A young woman's face stared back from within the frame—a nineteenth-century girl of the French provinces. A girl long dead, captured in this portrait by Van Gogh, simply titled "Girl in White." The young woman's face had a rare and riveting quality.

For one thing, her pure skin and dark hair were framed by a white hat that made the viewer focus on eyes that opened into an unfathomable soul. Was it a look of serenity— unbearable loss—or buried anger?

For another thing, the artist had used an *impasto* technique, dappling her white, form-fitting dress with thick dollops of paint. Surrounding her were raised globes of sunny coral, giving the impression of a poppy field in summer. Touching the paintings was prohibited, but Mary could never help herself when it came to this masterpiece. It wanted to be touched. Absently she reached out and ran one finger lightly over the canvas.

"I had a bet with myself that you'd do that," said a voice at her back.

Startled, Mary's hand snapped back to her side as she wheeled around.

The man was wearing jeans and a brown leather aviator's jacket. A green silk scarf at his throat, above an open-weave shirt, gave him a sophisticated, arty air. He looked to be in his late thirties, though the soft curls that touched his collar were heavily salted with gray.

He shrugged, saying with a cheerful, likable smile, "I can't resist her either."

Mary let out her breath. "You scared me. I feel like an art thief."

Boldly, as if they were acquainted, he stepped up beside her. Continuing to stare at the portrait, he said, "Pretty clever, what old Vince did. Don't you agree?"

"Yes," she replied carefully, without a clue as to what he meant.

"He captures the pure soul of a young woman. Then he dresses her up like this—so that anyone who sees her can't help wanting to do the forbidden thing and touch her. It's genius."

Mary was mulling over how she might slip away when the man tapped the fingertips of his right hand to his forehead. "I've been so rude, intruding on you like this. It's just that I feel like an old friend whenever I bump into a patron. You *have* been in, haven't you?"

"Been in where?" said Mary cautiously.

"To my gallery—over in Georgetown?" he replied. But when she showed no signs of recognition, his face fell.

"How embarrassing," he groaned. "I thought you were one of my patrons. My name's Mitch. I own a gallery. It's just—I don't know. Your style. Your obvious attraction to the best art. I mistook you. Please forgive me." He extended one hand apologetically.

Awkwardly, she shook his hand. "Sure. No problem." Actually, she was intrigued to meet a man who so obviously appreciated the soul of art, rather than the commercial aspects or the bottom line of an advertising budget.

Wanting to ease his embarrassment, Mary nodded at the portrait of the girl in white. "Do you really think that's what Van Gogh had in mind when he painted her?"

He smiled. "He was a desperately lonely man. She was innocent, vulnerable. I can tell by looking in the eyes. I don't know how he kept his hands off her," he said. "You like the Impressionists, I gather. Why?"

"They searched for the deeper meaning in things," she responded slowly, feeling pleased that he was interested in her opinion. "They have the power to carry you beyond the real, so you can sense the—the truth about things." Mary was afraid she was sounding like a freshman in art history. "I guess that sounds a little romantic."

"I'm a realist myself," he answered matter-of-factly. "As far as I can tell, this hard old world is all there is."

Noisy footsteps and giggles rounded the corner just then. The second graders.

With a wry smile and a touch of disgust, he said, "I can't figure out why they bring those noisy little monsters in here. There's enough gum stuck all over this gallery to hold the Soviet Union together."

Mary smiled, amused at his wit.

"Would you mind if I showed you another of my favorite paintings?" Mitch offered. "Where it's quiet?"

Mary could never remember exactly how the afternoon progressed from that point to a long conversation over espresso in a small cafe. Mitch's side of it was laced with fragments of poetry, sensitive insights, and insider stories about artists from New York to L.A. Fascinated, she never got back to the agency that day.

"You'll have to lie tomorrow, won't you?" Mitch smiled, shaking his finger at her.

She laughed. "It doesn't matter. Today—this

conversation—it was exactly what I needed. You have no idea. I can't believe we've talked for over four hours. I feel as if I've known you for so long. Like I've been high on something this afternoon."

Mitch shrugged. "Maybe you'll find it addicting."

Mitch's gallery was small but boasted a few works for sale by names Mary recognized. There were also a good many rather disturbing pieces by a Caribbean artist—huge canvases raked with agitated lines and extremes of color. It looked as if buckets of creosote had been dropped on one or two. Nor was the artist above using chicken blood. One painting even smelled strange.

Mary had only known Mitch for two weeks, so she reserved her comments.

"The artist practices voodoo," he explained as she stared at one of them. "She falls into trances and lets spirits paint through her. That's her claim anyway. It's not a bad hook when it comes to selling this stuff.

"She's still relatively unknown—but not for long. I've sold her to some high-placed government people. They don't know art, but they brag a lot. In fact, I think they hate the paintings. They just like to display the little card that explains their 'spiritual essence.' Whatever—her work's on the verge of becoming very pricey. Anyway, it's what I'm into right now.

"But," he added, "I'm always on the lookout for

new talent. I have a sixth sense about artists. I can feel who's going to connect with the collective unconscious of the art world."

Lightly, he touched Mary's shoulder. "Who knows. Maybe that's why I was drawn to you."

———

Mitch held Mary's sketch pad at arms' length. They were sitting on a bench in the little park at Dupont Circle. Mary waited nervously, listening to the splash of the fountain and the rush of traffic, while Mitch examined some drawings she'd done.

He put the pad down for a moment and looked at her, his jaw slack with amazement—then picked it up again, delicately, as if holding priceless Oriental paintings on rice paper.

"Astonishing," he said. "I can't believe we've known each other three months and you've withheld these sketches from me. One or two of them are so-so. But the rest are great!"

Mary wasn't sure they were that good. "You're being nice," she countered.

"No. Really. How can I convince you? This isn't mere talent. This is a gift. Incredible. What other works have you done? I have to see them. Please."

The next evening, Mitch came to her apartment for the first time. It had taken her this long—from spring till summer—to get up the courage or confidence to invite him home. During their time together, mostly dinner and theater dates, she'd been trying to figure out the mysterious quality about him. Sometimes he was confident, direct. Other times, she thought she sensed a wounded, retreating spirit. Even a cool and aloof air. It was Mitch's wounded, retreating side that drew her soul out to him.

He stood before her paintings for a long time. Sometimes he touched one canvas or the other with what seemed a cautious reverence. She sat on the sofa watching him, still enjoying the thrill of finding such a sensitive, intelligent friend. And she felt a cautious sense that maybe her future was finally opening before her.

"No one at your college saw how exceptional these are, did they?" When she shook her head, he slapped his thighs in a gesture of disbelief. "Those instructors—they were Philistines!

"We're going to arrange a show," he announced.

Mary sat up. "You're kidding. A show—of my works? I can't believe it. You know so many famous and sophisticated people—"

"Sophisticated," Mitch interrupted. "And that's the problem. To me, they've lost something. Here I see it again—innocence. It's irresistible. I could just consume it."

They talked late into the evening, discussing details of the exhibit and invitation lists of noted reviewers and critics and collectors, until Mary called a halt. "This is scaring me. It's a dream come true."

"Don't be afraid. I want to make your dreams come true," he said.

When Mitch left, after midnight, he took Mary's hands, pressed them together between his own—

his hands were so warm—and kissed her finger-tips. Brushing a strand of hair back from her cheek, he whispered:

> somewhere i have never travelled,
> gladly beyond
> any experience,
> your eyes have their silence . . . .

She gave him a curious look.

"E. E. Cummings," he explained. "You know—all those poems written in small letters. Like—'all in green went my love riding . . . 'four lean hounds crouched low and smiling.' He was a master of mood and impressions. What you do to me—it's like what I feel when I read one of his love poems."

He looked gently, directly, into her eyes and continued:

> your slightest look easily will unclose me
> though i have closed myself as fingers,
> you open always petal by petal myself as
>   Spring opens
> touching skillfully, mysteriously her
>   first rose . . .

> i do not know what it is about you that closes
> and opens; only something in me understands
> the voice of your eyes is deeper than all roses
> nobody, not even the rain, has such small
>   hands. . . .

Turning, he started down the stairs.

"Wait," she called after him, searching for words that would tenderly hold him. "I just—it's as if you know me the way no one else ever has. I want to say—if there's anything I can do to thank you for this kindness, all your care and encouragement—"

Mitch winced. "Don't. Please." And then he seemed to be searching for words, too.

"You're too beautiful, Mary," he said at last. "And I've been lonely for too long. I want to keep you on a pedestal—like a sculpture. A masterpiece. If you give me an opening like that again, I might suggest something that'll drive you away from me. And I couldn't stand that."

He turned and disappeared down the darkened stairwell.

After Mary closed the door, she moved quickly to the window. From there, she watched as a lone form in an aviator's jacket emerged on the empty sidewalk below and passed from the glow of one streetlight to another. Rounding a corner, he was gone.

A guilty thought sneaked in, one she'd never had about any man before. She wished he had stayed.

Nine

A brisk wind blew away the fog-phantom play from before her eyes. The woods was still, with an after-sunset lull.

The sudden loud sound, like crumpling cellophane or crunching ice, startled her. She'd fallen so deeply into her own thought-stream that she hadn't heard the approaching wall of freezing wind. It was nearly upon her, catching shreds of fog in its grip. The crumpling sound was actually mist freezing instantly into suspended plumes of ice crystal, like tiny cirrus clouds. Disoriented, she scrambled to escape the wind.

Skirting around the grove of dark pine trees, she came to a steep bank, stretching down. Bracing herself carefully from one tree to another, she made her way to the bottom. Here, the ground flattened out considerably and the trees grew even sparser. She'd be out in the open lands soon.

But what then?

To her left, in the evening dimness, mists rolled in runnels ahead of the wind—down toward the stream, most likely. Michael had told her to stay away from the stream, though. To bear to the right. He'd made a big point of that, she reminded herself, and said there was a passageway here.

To her right the trees thinned and the bank rose sharply beside her. At its base the ground was strewn with sharp rocks. Only about fifty yards from where she stood there appeared to be the opening to a passage, which she could just make out, cut into the far end of the cliff wall. By chance she glanced up.

She'd come to the base of another ridge, directly below the pine grove where she'd almost run into the hunter. Faintly she could see, at the top of the bank near the edge of the drop-off, a tall twisted pine. What caught her eye in this near-dark was the lightning scar down its length, and she drew a sharp breath.

The pale globe of light, which she'd mistaken for Michael's torch, had been leading her through the fog straight to this drop-off, where she would have fallen onto the deadly stones below.

If Michael hadn't saved me . . . she thought.

But at the same moment a doubt wormed in— or perhaps it shone like a gleam of clearer light. Wasn't it the hunter's appearance, at the last second, that caused her to halt? If he wanted to hurt her, if this had been a trap, then why had he interfered? He could have grabbed her, or even let her fall on these rocks.

But it was Michael who ran at me out of the fog, she argued with herself. *He pulled me away when the hunter was coming at me.*

Other thoughts kept trying to force upward from her subconscious, like lights from beyond a mental veil.

Michael makes you depend on him. Why is it that when you're with him, you wind up doubting what you think is right? She felt wretched and confused. *He erodes your confidence so you'll trust him—but that's not real trust. And if he wants your trust so much, why does he keep secrets from you? Isn't that what you've always hated—letting yourself be led blindly by someone, only to find out you were misled and that he really doesn't care about you at all, only himself?*

She hated when her mind did this. Why was she always miring herself in inner conflict? Tenderness and anger toward Michael wrangled within. When was she going to be a woman and break out of this turmoil? Stand on her own?

An all-too-familiar side whispered in response: *That's just it. You've never been able to think things through clearly and come to a good conclusion on your own. Why would you trust yourself now, when you're in the middle of a big mess like this?*

How can I be so ungrateful? she chided suddenly. *I keep doubting Michael. And at this very moment he's risking his life to lead that guy off my trail.*

The mysterious lights couldn't possibly be caused by anything human, of that she was sure. She'd been following a will-o'-the-wisp, some manifestation of nature. That was all. If she'd stepped over the rocky drop-off, it would have been an accident, her mistake and no one else's. And wasn't that the adult thing to do—to take responsibility for your own choices?

A low whine from the unrelenting wind, and the loud report of branches cracking in sleeves of ice, came from behind and moved her toward the opening in the rocks.

When she reached the passageway, she discovered that a second, narrower opening branched to the right, hugging tight against the stone wall of the drop-off. This second passage narrowed and narrowed until it was only a dark crack, which brought back the claustrophobic press of the cave. The wider opening obviously angled in the direction of the forest's outer edge.

She had just decided to take the wider way when the groan of timbers freezing and splitting began to explode close behind her. The wind wall had grown suddenly more violent, capturing the grove far above her with a vengeance. The front line of frost spread relentlessly over the last few pines, and was vining down the rocky drop-off.

The wind stiffened, whipping hair in her eyes. *I hope Michael makes it here in time!* she thought frantically. Why had he insisted she not wait?

Immediately inside the passage, the shadowed rock walls were more than arms' length apart. She hoped, as she hurried along, that there were no tight squeezes ahead. To her relief, the walls kept their distance, and she found herself moving at the bottom of a long, deep channel of stone—while far above, a starless sky foreshadowed the night.

This better be the right way, because once the opening is frozen shut, there'll be no other way to get out. I hope Michael wasn't wrong about this.

The floor of the canyon-like passage was free of stones and debris, so she was able to hurry. But her pace was controlled, allowing her to scan the enclosing walls for side passages or even large fissures leading out. *Out into what?* Maybe she would step through some narrow opening, like Alice through the looking glass, and simply find she'd startled herself awake on a sunny bench in downtown Washington.

She began to feel anxious. The mounting shriek of the wind's approach called after her, echoing down between the steep, unbroken walls. The passage kept turning left, but there was no sign of a way out.

Her mind was churning. *Michael said he'd find his way out of this place somehow if he didn't get here in time to meet me. Is there another way out? Why didn't he tell me about it?*

One more turn, and the passage stopped.

A dead end.

Panicked, she began to backtrack. If there was a way out through this passage, she'd missed it. But she'd been so careful.

Breaking into a run, she searched for a crack or fissure. Anything that looked like a way out. The walls remained unforgivingly solid.

It can't be, she argued with herself. But it had to be true. She should have taken the other passage. Maybe there was still time.

Near the opening, the passage veered sharply, and she nearly collided with a shadowed figure.

Michael seized her by the shoulders, looking startled, or angry. A roar of dark wind nearly toppled them both.

"I came as soon as I could!" he shouted over the blast. "He was harder to shake than I thought."

"Which—way?" Mary shouted back.

He pointed back the way she'd just come. "In there."

The ice wall was already sealing the entrance to the other passage, not twenty feet away.

"There's no way out!" she yelled.

He grabbed her by one wrist, pulling her back into the passage. "Why didn't you keep going as I told you?"

"It's a dead end. This is a mistake!" she shouted, resisting him.

He turned on her, eyes hard with irritation. "We don't have time to argue about this. There *is* a way. You just missed it."

"If one of us doesn't use his head," she yelled, "we'll both be dead!"

"Then I'll do the thinking! You shut up and do just what I tell you."

If he had dropped a match in a crate of dynamite, the result could not have been more violent. A fire went wild inside Mary. Wrenching her arm from his grip, she shoved him against the wall. "Let me go!" As he fell, she turned to run.

The rage of ice and wind was near. Devouring.

A massive glacier of deathly cold threatening to close the entrance.

As she bolted for freedom, a fresh blast of wind threw her hard against a wall. It roared like death in her ears. She staggered. Caught herself. Wind poured like fluid frost into the passage, half-sealing the entrance now.

Michael was on his feet again, grabbing for her. "You're crazy!" he yelled above the roar.

She tore loose, lunging, shutting her eyes against the fierce cold that burned her face. And slipping through the opening, she was out. Half-tripping, half-blown, she ran before the gale force.

Wind carried his words, like scattering leaves, "Stay . . . away . . . from . . . stream!"

She never looked back.

The stream was exactly where she would go.

Even in the gathering, deepening twilight she sensed the direction. Only weariness tried to hold her back; the weariness of too-long fending for herself. A whole lifetime of pain and soul-sickness wanted to wrap ghostly arms around her and pull her down in its embrace. A woolly faintness made her face and hands tingle, but she drove herself on.

All this time she'd gone along with Michael's insistence that she avoid the stream. Why? Because he was a man? Because she'd always trusted a man's words more than her own instincts?

Yet at the moment she had broken away from his grip, one thought drove her: She'd gone against her own intuitions for the last time. Too long she'd given other people the power to make choices for her. It had been safer that way. And if anything went wrong, she didn't have to take responsibility—she could blame someone else.

Courage to listen to the voice within had first come when she was trapped in the cave. Like a woman drowning, she gripped that courage now. Somehow in this place she was being forced to face, and to make, her own choices.

The stream. She had to reach it. Had to know why she held this certainty that the way through the center of this nightmare was the way of escape.

At the bottom of the great bowl of wilderness, the light was so poor all the trees faded together, their branches little more than charcoal lines against gray paper. The ghostliness was palpable, and she felt like nothing more than a passing spirit.

The moment she came to the stream brought a trumpet of elation—which died away in an instant.

Instead of pacing along in its lively glide, the water had run into mucky lowlands and slowed to a drag. In the crook of a tree root, along the bank, a gray-brown scum collected. Beyond this, by maybe a stone's throw, the sluggish stream widened into a marsh. The water gave off a stagnant odor.

Had she only imagined it all this time—the light within this water? No. Liquid clouds of brightness still floated in its depths, even though much of the red-gold light had dimmed from the distant sky.

Where is this light coming from? What is it trying to tell me?

Weakly, she sank down beside the sluggish, stinking water—half-willing, half-fearing what it would call up. . . .

———

. . . Olivia had phoned to invite Mary "home" for the weekend after Christmas. When she responded that she and Mitch had plans for New Year's Eve, Olivia was insistent, saying that she really wanted to see her. But she refused, however, to say what was on her mind, no matter how much Mary pressed her.

When Mary arrived the next Friday evening, Olivia seemed exceptionally cordial as she took Mary's coat at the door.

"Where's the silver calling card tray?" Mary teased her. "The next time I come, I'm going to expect valet parking."

Olivia kissed her lightly on the cheek and smiled. "Why don't you go in and sit down. I've been keeping dinner warm."

The dining room only added to the air of mystery. Candles shed a soft steady light over two perfect place settings of crystal and silver and fine china. On a plate in the center of the white tablecloth—a gift from Mary herself at Olivia's recent bridal shower—was a small loaf of bread, covered with a linen napkin. Mary ran her finger along the rim of one dinner plate.

"Mags, this is your wedding china!" she said as Olivia came through the doorway with a steaming roast. "Shouldn't you be saving this for your first dinner with Harlan after the wedding?"

Olivia kept the conversation to small talk through most of the meal. When they had both finished, she went to the sideboard and gathered up a plate, a single crystal glass and a tall crystal decanter filled with a rich burgundy liquid. She brought these to the table and sat down again.

Mary watched intently as Olivia poured. Candlelight bled through the glass and rocked in a red disk against the tablecloth.

Uncovering the plate of bread, Olivia wordlessly offered it to her friend. Then, the first sip of the cup.

When they finished, Olivia looked almost relieved. For a long while, neither said a word.

"Thanks, Mags. That was lovely," Mary offered at last. "I was almost expecting that you'd set me up for a date with Walker this weekend."

"Why on earth did you think that?"

"Because you keep reminding me how often he asks about me. And because I know you and Harlan don't really like Mitch."

"We never said that."

"You don't have to say anything. I could tell how the two of you felt about him when you came to Washington at Thanksgiving for my show. From the minute you walked into Mitch's gallery I knew you were uncomfortable."

"You have to admit, that Caribbean lady with the dreadlocks and filthy two-inch fingernails was from the dead zone," Olivia smiled, rolling her eyes.

"I meant the way you reacted to Mitch. Remember, I know 'southern politeness' when I see it. Give him a chance, Mags. I know he acted pretty rude to that woman who brought her two kids to the show. But his life is art—kids just aren't on his agenda. He has some kind of phobia about them. I can live with that."

When Olivia did not reply, Mary smiled at her. "You'll really like him when you get to know him better. Come on. I thought you'd be happy that I've finally found someone who cares about me as much as Mitch does."

Olivia's dark eyes searched Mary's face, and she seemed troubled. Then, reaching across the table, she laid one hand on top of Mary's.

"Mary, I know what's happening between you and Mitch."

Mary sat back. A coldness came over her, settling in the pit of her stomach. Tears rose, but she fought them back. She could only say, after a moment, "How did you know?"

"I can't really say—I just knew. I guess I first realized it on the drive home that weekend of your exhibit. I haven't said anything to Harlan. You're my friend, my sister, Mary, and I wanted to keep this between you and me. If you want to talk, I want to listen."

Though it was painful, Mary told her everything. About the first lonely evening she'd given in to Mitch's touch, even though he'd never said a word, never pressed himself on her. Mitch had not asked her to move in, but they were spending most weekends together at his apartment.

"But I can't blame Mitch. It was me, Olivia. I made the choice. I practically threw myself at him and said, 'Take me home.' And I can't believe it.

"Remember me in high school, Mags? I'm the one who stayed away from girls who were 'easy.' I'm the one who avoids other women in the agency because they sleep around. Now look at me—the great hypocrite." Dry sobs were shaking her so hard she could not go on.

"I had a little sermon all thought out," said Olivia, "with Scripture quotes and everything. But I've chucked it. I'm just going to talk—straight-talk.

"It scares me, what you're doing, Mary. I have a terrible feeling you're going to be so destroyed when this is over."

Mary stared at her, stunned into silence.

"You may be furious with me for saying this, but I'm telling you—I don't trust Mitch. Not for a minute. You think you made that choice all on your own. In one way that's true—and in another way it's not. He's an 'artist' all right, and he's manipulating you."

"No," Mary objected, shaking her head. "Mitch really loves me, like no one else I've ever known. Ever. In my whole life. Maybe you can't understand this, but he gives me what I've always needed inside."

"What is that?" Olivia asked gently.

The question stopped Mary dead in her tracks. She realized that she didn't really have an answer. Then she hedged, "I can't say exactly. I guess it's love—at least love as I understand it. He thinks my art is going to take off. He treats me like a queen. I'm hooked." And after another pause, "You may be surprised to know that Mitch even went to church with me on Christmas."

They talked into the early hours of the morning. And the next afternoon Mary invented a reason to drive back to Washington early, although she herself raised the subject of Mitch as she was leaving.

"Maybe my feelings about right and wrong have changed. Maybe love is what's right. I don't know. That part confuses me. Maybe I just have to find it out for myself—make my own mistakes."

"Why?" Olivia challenged. She seemed more agitated now than the evening before. "Did you hear what you just said? Why go on if you know it's a mistake? Mary, break off with him. Please. You can't see it, but you're in the grip of something that's only going to hurt you in the end—emotionally and spiritually."

Mary did not respond but slipped her coat on. "Do you still want me as your maid of honor? Your guests might see the scarlet A. I mean, am I still welcome here?"

"Stop it, Mary!" Olivia shot back. "That's not what I mean. You know I'll always love you. Don't become a stranger to me." The pleading in her voice made something tighten in Mary's throat. As she opened the door, Olivia suddenly hugged her. Then she stood back, clasping Mary's shoulders with both hands, and looked straight into her eyes. "I only want you to do one small thing. Promise?"

"What is it?"

"You said you were confused. Mary—don't get angry—I believe you feel that way because you're running from some things. If you'd just let yourself sit still long enough to listen, you'd begin to hear the truth.

"So when you get home tonight, don't call Mitch. Just get alone and get quiet. I believe God can speak to you, even through all the confusion. Take a piece of paper and write down—honestly— whatever comes. Promise?"

Mary gave her an odd look.

———

It took several cups of tea and a long wait, and Mary realized it was the first time in months that she'd been alone without switching on the radio or television to fill in the silence.

Finally she felt herself crossing that inner border an artist recognizes, into a clear sense of how she related to things. She took up a pencil, and words strung themselves out in black lines.

> Two ghosts
> met on a bannister,
> a moon-brushed narrow newelpost,
> on branches
> cracking in sleeves of ice,
> on a sheaf of wind

One
tied the milky way,
a ribbon,
vague or lovely
in her hair

One
used the strong speech—
flattery—
and promises like shadows

And hell
was in their void embrace

Mary set down her pencil and scanned the page.
She read the lines three times.

Later, when she'd gone to bed, the paper lay on
the floor, crumpled. . . .

"I'm an artist—that's why," Mitch replied,
barely keeping the irritation from his voice.

Mary could make no sense of what he was telling her, or why he'd suddenly become so harsh.
"What does being an artist have to do with truly
loving each other? With wanting to be committed
to each other?"

"Because marriage isn't love. Marriage binds
you. Kids tie you down."

"How?" she pressed. "How does marriage and
a family tie you down? That doesn't make sense—

not if you've found the person you want to love forever."

"You're beginning to sound like you write grade-B movie dialogues," Mitch threw back. Then, "Wait a minute. You're not trying to hint at something, are you? You're not—"

Mary recovered enough to fix him with a smile. "No. Don't be ridiculous."

"That's good," Mitch replied, with obvious relief. "Look, I'm sorry I reacted so strongly, Mary. But I know how women are. They want assurances. A home. Kids. All that traditional stuff. That's not me.

"I believe in simple trust, Mary. So you'll just have to trust my love—that it will always be there for you, even if you can't hold on to me with a signed, sealed piece of paper. Just trust me. You see how empty your ideas about commitment are, don't you?"

"Yes," she smiled again, trying to cover for her sinking heart, "I do see."

Ten

The current floated a drift of foam scum past her sight. Cold poured down the funneling wilderness. Behind her the trees' groan mingled with the pitch and howl of the wind's thousand voices, like lost souls caught in a storm.

Dumbstruck and staring, she sat rooted beneath the weight of revelation that was bursting in upon her. Olivia had been right. Right about so many things. More than that, her friendship had been a communion of truth and love.

She felt a hot surge of embarrassment at her own blindness, and she resisted. *I only wanted someone to love. Was that so wrong? Mitch loved me.*

But her weak argument was futile, and she knew it. Real love and its living language of truth was making too much clear, cutting away the snaring wires of old lies.

It wasn't blindness, an inner voice challenged her. *Blindness means you can't see. But you willfully, deliberately refused to see what Mitch was like. You wouldn't face the truth about him.*

The ironic thing was that with each new and deeper burst of revelation, another weary, soul-sick layer lifted and drifted away, *Like the ragged bits of scum floating off downstream.*

What about the terrible things that were done to me? What about the people who did them? she wanted to rage.

Even as the accusations welled up, they were driven back as a stark bravery came to replace the sick fear. *It doesn't matter, right now, what was done to you. You've been brought to this place, alone, to face what you have done.*

She wanted to object, but could not. It was true.

She had buried one secret act—a painful, ugly thing that she'd suppressed from the daylight of her mind. Maybe it was this act that made her soul a haunted place, where she would be brought to ground by a lone demon of judgment. Her own excuses and accusations had fallen, like so many faded leaves, to bury the truth.

Now the wind was coming. She had to cross the marsh. And beyond that—what?

She'd run from Michael, following the inner sense that she must find her own way through the heart of this wild darkness. Now, from behind, the ice was closing in, and she knew the time and place of reckoning were very near.

There was no going back. She'd made her choice, running—stupidly or otherwise—from Michael's promise of escape. Ahead, in the darkness, must be one last well of memory. Had the hunter driven her to this?

At least if you're honest with yourself for once,
she thought, *you may find some peace—when the
end comes.*

An air of ancient decay hung above the oily-dark
poolings of water that collected around stands of
cattails, bent-broken like so many spider legs. In
the center of the marsh, a small rise of ground sup-
ported the remnants of a dead tree. Its bark hung
in gray tatters, like skin peeled back to reveal whi-
tened and cracked-off bones.

She carefully set out for this high point, across
spongy hummocks of graying grass, the inky muck
sucking at her feet as if to pull her into itself. The
evil smelling water, darker than strong tea,
brought to mind a photo essay she had seen in a
nature magazine. An ancient people, for fear of sav-
age gods, had bound men and women and cast
them, live victims, into a peat bog. Murder—to
keep themselves in the gods' good graces.

*What kind of an inhuman being could think
up such a terrible way to kill another human?* she
had wondered at the time.

From beneath this sullen water, she thought
she saw faces in contortion. They implored her
with their eyes, and accused her. Not the faces of
men and women, but small, sorrowful faces.

The secret began to scrape its way to freedom,
like a tiny fingernail, from the hollow, aching place
within.

The little island turned out to be a low hump of huge rock, barely skinned over with a dry, brittle matting of moss and grass. Beneath the skeletal tree, cupped into the stone, was a shallow pool, small as a baptismal font, its water strong with the rotting smell of death.

The ache in her stomach was greater than a pain remembered; it had intensified into a piercing agony. So much that she'd begun to pant for air, her mouth dry and parched. It was this pain that knocked her to her knees before the little pool.

Am I strong enough to do this?

She forced her eyes to turn down, into the lifeless water . . .

. . . Late March in Washington brought a series of the kind of days when the cold air is pierced by warm sharp rays of strengthening sunlight. On one of these days, Mary drove out past the greening fields west of the city and into a small town. She had a morning appointment, and she was early.

Two thoughts gnatted around her mind.

Go back and call Olivia. She'll help you.

Purposely, though, she had not called Olivia in the three months since that last dinner together— first, because Olivia might be disappointed in her and, second, because of the other harassing thought.

You're an adult, and you got yourself into this mess. No one else can get you out.

Never had she felt so miserably alone. Only

much later would she identify the numbness that, for several weeks, had been spreading itself over her soul—a feeling that she was coming to the final curtain of her life before its first act was over.

This glacial advance of despair had begun creeping in with her first suspicion five weeks ago, when she had missed her period the second time. Sometimes she missed one, but never two in a row. Two home tests proved what she did not want to believe.

Casually—or as casual as she could make it sound—Mary had floated a hint in Mitch's direction. His response told her he wanted marriage, a home and a baby as much as he wanted a rusty nail run through his foot.

So she had kept her secret. Mitch could never know. He might be angry. He might leave her.

She had phoned and scheduled an appointment at a country hospital an hour's drive from the city. That way there would be no chance at all of awkwardly running into a friend or a client of the agency. No one would ever know.

Pulling into the hospital lot, she fixed her mind on a single hypnotic thought. As her heels clicked across the blacktop, through the glass door, and down the quiet, polished hallways, she repeated: *I'm doing what's best for everyone.*

An older woman in a white lab coat led her to a small cubicle office, where a counselor noted Mary's responses on a clipboard.

Was this her first time?

"Yes."

What about medications, allergies, family histories of . . . .

"No . . . no . . . no."

Was she sure of her decision?

"Yes."

Please sign here.

A nurse led her to a changing room. Mary slipped into a hospital gown, feeling cold and shaky—and then into the "procedure room," as the nurse called it.

"You may experience some discomfort," she said as Mary lay back on the table. "It doesn't last long, though. Just do the deep breathing the counselor showed you. Keep it slow and even so you don't hyperventilate. If you need someone, just press the call button in your room."

The doctor examined her, checked her questionnaire, and looked at the nurse. He'd barely spoken to Mary at all, and it was strange how he talked over her to the nurse. "This says she thinks she's as much as ten weeks along. I'd say she's fourteen to sixteen weeks. I take it this is her first time."

"Do you want to go with saline?" the nurse asked him.

"I think that's the safest route."

After the injection, Mary was taken to a room and left alone. She repeated her single calming thought "This is best for everyone" until the first pains tightened her abdomen. A bead of cold perspiration trickled down one temple.

Before she could prevent it, a small smooth-skinned face swam up through her thoughts. Mary clenched her eyes against the tears—clenched her heart against the too-late remorse.

She imagined, within, tiny arms and legs flailing. The saline was already doing its work. *Why did I do this. . . ?*

Terrific pain seized her abdomen now, and she silently commanded herself: *Breathe! Focus on breathing.*

When the contraction passed, she was shaking. The soulful little face, with pleading eyes and perfect lips, like a porcelain doll, focused in her mind's eye as if asking, *Why?*

Another kick of pain moments later forced Mary to breathe, forced her thoughts to drown the pleading face. She had to grip the bedrail to keep from crying out.

For several hours, between erratic seizures of pain, Mary kept fighting one miserable thought: *This is the price you have to pay.*

It was late in the afternoon before she finally pressed the button, summoning help. Shifts had changed. She didn't recognize the nurse's aide who rushed in and stood at her side, squeezing her hand.

With a few pushes, Mary delivered her baby into a steel laboratory pan.

When she was done, the woman said, "Please turn your head for a moment." Then she carried the tray out for disposal.

Mary was grateful she'd seen nothing.

The aide returned. "Just rest now," she said. "I see you came alone, so take all the time you need.

You'll be amazed how strong you feel in a little bit."

Two more days of bed rest at home blurred together.

On the third day, back at work and sitting at her drawing table, Mary watched color flow across the blank paper. The hand holding the pen moved as if disconnected from her body. Flawless sketches and layouts seemed to spill from someone else's creativity.

But in her stomach, Mary cradled an empty ache. And during the long nights after, she could not wipe clean the memory, or ease the burning. . . .

. . . On this island of cold stone, the dead tree keeping lonely vigil, Mary sat lost in the wilderness of her own mortally wounded soul.

The exquisite pain had passed, leaving her wrung out, drenched with guilt at her cold-hearted choice. She had sacrificed her own baby for Mitch.

Michael had told her this was a place of reckoning, and deep within she had always known what the reckoning was about. But from the first she'd held on to the hope that she could reason with someone, that she could escape judgment.

How could she have hoped for even a whisper of understanding or forgiveness for what she'd done?

Wretched beyond all hope, Mary stared at the death-poisoned font. Then, from the corner of her eye, she caught it—the faintest wick of light, as if the water had one final thing to tell her . . .

. . . A week after her "corrective surgery"—as Mary called it—she had visited a friend in the hospital. She felt like a statue visiting the living. As she was leaving, just before stepping outside into the early April evening, she was drawn toward a soft light spilling from a small door at one end of the lobby.

A small chapel contained a few wooden benches and heavy red carpet that led down a narrow aisle to an altar table. Behind that, a pale curtain draped the front wall, and at the center hung a simple wooden cross. Except for low, indirect lighting, the room was dim.

In the center of the table burned one tall white candle. On this feather of light, Mary fixed her eyes.

She knelt before it, crushed beneath her secret burden. Mitch would never know. Olivia would never know. She alone would carry the secret to her grave—of that she was resolved.

She knelt a long time. It was hopeless to pray, though, and the sacred atmosphere began to weigh on her.

All her life she'd felt separated from any greater power that might give her so much as a second thought. But never had she felt this completely cut off. It was as if in the dim atmosphere of the chapel unseen hands were smothering the candlelight.

How could she pray? What right did she have to cry out across the chasm she felt inside?

Stiffly, as if she were an old woman with little life left in her bones, Mary got up to leave.

The candle burned unwaveringly.

Suddenly Mary dropped back onto her knees, hiding her face in her hands. From her last crumbling edge of hope, her soul cried out in agony.

Jesus! . . .

———

. . . Mary was barely aware of making her way out of the marsh, and felt only the slightest relief in escaping the forest she'd entered a lifetime ago.

When the wind shrieked up to the back edge of the marsh, she'd wanted to wrap her arms around the trunk of the tree and let the burning cold seize her at last. Why run if there was no escape? But that final flicker of memory was trying to tell her something—not only about her life-remembered but the reason she'd been brought to this wilderness behind the world. Either that or she simply did not have the courage to die after all.

She raced down through the dark, barely ahead of the cold-moving wall of death devouring everything behind her.

The stream rushed beside her again, panicked in its flight, carrying a burnished-copper glow from the perishing light above. The blackness of coming night pressed in, swiftly, as time and light came speeding to a close. And memories, those relentless, funereal mourners of the soul, kept treading—treading—until it seemed her senses would break through. And space itself began to toll.

Up ahead, there loomed a spectral sight.

When she had seen this skyline from a distance, it had held an illusive, veiled look. Now she could see that, in fact, it was not like any natural sky she had ever known. What towered ahead of her, thick and looming and formidable as a battlement, yet translucent, was a curtain of light, thick with a many-colored luminescence against the oncoming billows of blackness.

Resting beneath this curtain, seemingly cut in half by it, lay an ink-black sea. She had not seen this from the distance, for it had been concealed in darkness.

When she reached the shore of this lost sea, she could go no farther. The black waters spread out in both directions. Standing at its very brink, she looked out over the obsidian surface. Lights bled through the great dividing veil, floating in weird watery ribbons of yellow, red, blue, and shadings of purple—as if from some tremendous blaze on the other side.

For a moment, all was deathly silent, the air undisturbed by even a breath of wind. It no longer mattered what happened to her, she thought dully. The wind and ice and blackness would finally capture her here. Already her breath was coming in cloud-puffs, and she pulled her jacket tight.

So this is where it ends, she thought, past caring. *Alone. In this freezing darkness.*

Despite Michael's rudeness, his unnerving swings between arrogance and appeal, she wished he were at her side now. But she had pushed him away, made him stumble and fall in the passage-way. Maybe she was responsible for his death, too.

Close behind, the dust began to billow and roll before the cold driving wind. Lightnings flared in the sulphurous-red dark—some pale, some flinch-ingly sharp. The storm broke with rumblings, like two maelstroms in debate, shaking the ground.

Suddenly the last vestige of warm air was draw-ing out in a current, like an ocean tide rushing away, into the hollow front gathering before the storm's fury. And then, in its place, came the first rushing edge of bitter cold. As it struck, the black mirror of water crimped and riffled in the upsurg-ing airs, scattering in colors.

A fork of lightning jolted the air—made her duck and shield her eyes.

Then two figures were approaching, driven on the face of the storm. Running toward her, as if out of the wind itself, was Michael. Behind him came the hunter.

Rushing to her side, Michael poised himself protectively. Glaring at the hunter. "You stay away from her!" he shouted. "She's with me."

The hunter had stopped several yards away, showing no signs of threat. For the first time, she could see his face clearly. After all her curiosity, he was disappointingly plain. He hung back, waiting, leaning the strong beam of his shoulders against the wind.

"Let her come to me," he said, commanding. "You can't stop her, not if she wants to come." It seemed as if he was actually holding back the storm, as if the wild-blown clouds hesitated.

"How did you get out of that passage?" she hissed in Michael's ear. "I barely made it out myself."

He shot her an irritated look and replied, "You should have stayed with me."

She stood her ground. "I had to decide my own way for once. And if I'm so irritating to you, why did you come after me?"

A magnificent range of expressions surged across his face, from anger to loving exasperation. "Because I couldn't let you face this alone. Even if you are stubborn."

This almost threw her. "If you mean the 'reckoning' you've been talking about, I've decided to face whatever is coming to me. It can't be worse than the hell I've been through—can it?" she said, the cold biting at, weakening, her conviction.

Michael flashed an inscrutable look at the hunter, who continued to withstand the wind as it struck at his shoulders and back. "Can't you see," he said, "he's been driving you. Wearing you down. So you'll go crawling to him. I won't let you do it. You have no idea what's on the other side of this water. It would have been better if you had let yourself die back there than to—"

"Die?" she broke in. "You said that passage was a way out. All along you've been promising to help me escape and—"

"What he's trying to do," the hunter suddenly broke in, "is to interfere with my plans for you. But," he said, turning his attention to Michael, "this is as far as you can go. I told you there was a limit."

Mary was looking back and forth between both men, startled and anxious. "You know each other? What's going on here, Michael?"

The hunter smiled. "Go ahead. Tell her, Michael—and I can't believe you had the nerve to use that name. Just remember, however you try to influence her this time—whether you tell the truth, or lie, or confuse the two as usual—the decision is hers. You've worked a long time to keep her from me. But she's listened to you long enough. You can't stop her from coming across with me now. Not if that's what she wants."

Michael's pale blue eyes and handsome features turned to her, appealing. "Don't be unfair to me, Mary. I love you," he said, pitifully. "I loved you when I first saw you. Can't you tell he's trying to separate us? Okay, so I made one bad move back there when I tried to force you. You're harboring some bitterness toward men—I've felt it all along—but don't let that turn you against me now."

Mary wavered, hating herself for it. And she hated the fact that Michael, or whoever he was, appeared to be eagerly counting on her indecision.

"Don't you think it's time to stop being the wounded little girl?" Michael made a final bid for her sympathies, imploring, the muscles of his neck drawn like bowstrings. "Forget all those other men who've hurt you. Trust me, Mary. I only want what's best for you."

What it was that determined Mary's decision,

she would never fully remember. Maybe it was the hunter's clear, honest laughter at Michael's final plea. Maybe it was her own new conviction that what was best for her was probably beyond human knowing. She'd certainly seen, in her heart of hearts, that true motives could become confused with lying ones.

And she hated Michael's skill at bending her will to his own—she saw that now. He was too much like all the men who'd tricked her before.

But the strongest influence of all was the decision she'd already made: If she had been brought here to pay for her crime, she would not run from it any longer.

Even if her voice lacked strength, she said, determined, "You're right, Michael. It's time to stop being the wounded little girl. It amazes me that you know so much about my past, though I'm afraid to ask how you know it.

"But I've already trusted you. And when things went wrong, you made me feel as if it was my fault—my mistake. You've played with my mind. And the disgusting thing is, I think I suspected it all along and let you do it.

"No—I'm not going to stay here with you. I can't. Don't say anything or try to stop me. I'm willing to face whatever comes. I've made bad choices, but I believe this is a good one. I can't undo what I've done, but at least facing it is my choice and not someone else's. Maybe this won't make sense to you, but that feels good for a change."

The storm rose again, shrill, and the ground

began to frost and heave in the death-surge of ice.

She dashed to the hunter's side and was surprised to see that, up close, the plain face was somehow alarming—solemn and good, and yet forbidding. Maybe this was a mistake . . . The icy blast pressed them to the edge of the black water, and surges of spray flew wildly on the storm. Michael was left straining against the harsh wind.

She looked at the hunter anxiously, questioningly.

"We cross over here," he said in reply.

Then he bent and caught her up behind her knees and shoulders. Holding her firmly, he stepped into the black water, which came barely to his ankles.

When she looked down, however, it seemed as if she were being carried out over a chasm of lightless, bottomless, eternal night.

With the freezing cold pressing behind, and the bright veil before, he waded out toward the middle. Suddenly he was up to his hips, the water splashing her feet. Liquid blackness reached up to seize her in its arms, reflecting in its wild surges the lights that were like flames up the veiling sky.

Too late, she realized the hunter was pulling her down beneath the water. Fearfully she began to struggle, but he clamped her tighter in his arms.

At the last second she caught one glimpse of the solitary figure back on the freezing shore. He seemed alight with a pale glow—but that may only have been some reflection of the wild and surging storm lights.

Above the wind's howl, he was shouting bitterly that she was an idiot for not listening to him.

Eleven

Mary's struggle in the hunter's grip, as he took her down into the deep water, was only for a moment. With supreme effort she held her survival instincts in check, forcing herself to lie still in his arms.

Water seeped behind her clenched eyelids and down her throat, its saltiness burning, gagging. The pressure beat in her ears. He carried her deeper still. She tightened her lips, conserving the last little treasure of air. Her head pounded. Her lungs begged. They ached, then could no longer resist.

Quitting the fight at last, Mary let herself breathe in. And was amazed that there was no in-pull of water.

Her eyes came open in surprise—and without the sting of salt water. She was not beneath a black sea, but afloat in a bathing white light that swirled in images and prismatic colors.

She found herself staring upward through a rippled glassiness into the searching green eyes of a blond girl of about eight, who was taking refuge in a lonely woods. Drifting in perfect calm below the wind-raked translucence that divided them, the older Mary discovered herself thinking the young Mary's thoughts.

I promise I'll never love anyone besides you.

But now Mary could also hear beyond that one vow with its noble intention. She could listen through all the embittering months and years as the girl grew and took the shape of a woman, the bruised child still buried in her heart. It was like watching a sliver work beneath skin, slowly covering over with callousing layers, and later causing mysterious, hidden pains and festers.

She heard the submerged heart-words she had never even thought aloud to herself, words that had bound her into misdirected choices.

Oliver's sweet care made me feel beautiful and worthy of love.

The sensitive love of a man is the only thing that can make me feel worth anything.

Without the high and pure and perfect love I need, nothing else matters. Life isn't worth living.

Above all else, I must be loved.

And she understood many other things.

All along she'd blamed Wallace's abuse for her desperate love-need—but that was only partly true. In reality, she'd already enshrined her idea of a "perfect" love before Wallace battered his way in. Afterward, she had shut and bolted the door to her heart, so that no one except a dream prince of her own making would ever be allowed to enter. Wallace's abuse had never caused the need, only deepened her demand for it, slowly twisting her natural desire for love into something unnatural.

Only another unnatural force could then lead her out of the overgrown forest of her overly romantic notions about men. Only an unnatural light of wisdom could find its way into the tangled wilderness of her heart, causing her to see that no human has the power to bring into the soul of another the high and eternal joy for which it thirsts.

She now understood that she had fallen in love with love, had lost herself in self. She'd refused to see the men she'd desired as they truly were. Instead, she chose to dream-coat every imperfection, hoping to find a perfect love. One perfect pearl.

The ugly truth, anchored in concealing blackness at the floor of her soul, was this: She had not sacrificed anything for Mitch. It was for her own self that she had destroyed her baby. She'd cast her own soul like dice, gambling for a sick love against eternal damnation.

All of this Mary *knew* in a blaze of revelation. These were truths she would have rejected from anyone else, but the steady hand of grace was revealing them to the innermost core of her being.

The adult Mary—lavered with light, shot through with light—faced herself: The eight-year-old, who was prisoned within, was bathed and softened and loosed to go free.

And in that moment her desire for a false, princely dream-god died.

It was some time before she was aware that the hunter had let her slip from his arms.

He had completed his careful mission. He had helped her find her way—using even the diabolical schemes of her false guide—to come to this sea of her own bitter, unwept tears. He had bathed her in its warm, salty waters to expose and cleanse the festering wound of pride. His job completed, this guide and friend of the lost whispered something in her ear and was gone.

Tides of a brilliant whiteness blinded Mary's eyes shut again. The flood carried her along.

Still agonizing at her sin, she was oblivious that the salt tide of a lifetime's tears was turning fresh and sweet—and barely aware that waves were rocking her like comforting arms as she drifted upward.

Twelve

She stood on the shore of a crystal sea. Though the sun was not yet up, the new morning air was warm and alight with brilliant colors.

Her first thoughts were of the hunter. There was no trace of him.

Only his whispered words remained: *"I've led you to the truth. Now I'm going away for a bit. But don't worry. I'm getting some things ready for you, and in a little while you'll see me again."* She didn't know what to make of these words that raised a timid hope in her heart.

But wasn't a punishment due?

Looking back, she saw that a wintry rage was still blowing on the far side of the water. The violent storm front had stopped at the sea's mid-point, where it formed a dramatic skyline of purple-black billows, creased with blood-colored lights. Beyond it, the opposite shore—the open lands, forests, and mountain—dismaled away into gray, dying distance. Everything that had happened to her on that other side, and all that was revealed to her while passing beneath the waters, was still vivid in her mind. But now it was like looking back on the misery of it through an oily-dark glass, as if it had happened in another lifetime.

By contrast, the nearer half of the sea and the air above it shimmered, demanding to be filled with living things and the song of spring. Mary expected to see arcing dolphins, leaping otters, and silver-flashing fish in the water, or white birds circling in the nimble and waking blue sky.

A joyful little stream flowed out beside her, and when she caught sight of herself in its clear surface, she was even more amazed!

Gone were the twill slacks and quilted jacket, torn and soiled from all her groping and struggling. Instead, she was gowned in a fabric she'd never seen anywhere—blue as truth, red as love, with a thread of royal purple sketching throughout. She looked radiant, dignified—imperial.

Mostly, though, she wondered at the wordless joy that clothed her heart; she felt nearly weightless.

And this new land! It fanned out from the sea like a living brighter mirror-image of the wilderness she'd left. A bowl of grassland swooped up and away toward the edge of a silver forest awash with pale greens and the first white hint of blossoms. Above, a mountain's massive shoulders tapered up into the first lights of day, which trumpeted silently from behind its soaring peak.

So these were the lights she had seen from the dying autumn side of the wilderness. She realized, astonished, that she'd mistaken the announcement of a long-awaited dawn for the day's end. But why was it so very long in coming?

I feel as if I've come through a nightmare, and now I'm in a fantastic dream. I definitely don't deserve to feel this wonderful, she thought with guilt and sadness. *It's going to feel so terrible when I have to face whatever judgment I have coming.*

On the mountaintop a faint green glow colored the sky, growing until the peak was crowned with an emerald rainbow. From the center of the rainbow, a white halo of light flashed and broke from the circle, cutting a dazzling line like the brilliant point of a welder's torch, moving swiftly down the slopes.

At the same moment, a song of intricate harmony flooded the air—a music caught by no human ear, but only by a heart in tune. Like an anthem it rose, making Mary's stomach leap, announcing the approach of some magnificent presence.

Now the lower forest flashed with the white light, coming nearer, lancing at her from the trees, which seemed to bow aside, allowing it to pass. The air roared with thunderings that galloped down the open land directly toward her. Where it passed, the landscape was rinsed in brilliance.

And then, at the center of the moving spark of light, she saw him! Clothed in sunlight, a man riding on a white horse. Lightning splashed from flashing hooves as horse and rider thundered closer, closer, down to the shore, and reined to a halt where Mary stood.

She stared, afraid and hopeful, at the magnificent man who sat regarding her, silently, with searching eyes.

He was powerfully built, broad-shouldered, and firm-handed with the splendid horse, which champed impatiently beneath him. Dressed in snowy white finery, the man carried himself with the bearing of royalty, a prince in courtly splendor. Yet there was humility and even sorrow in his steady look.

A gold sash fell diagonally from one shoulder, across a chest that might have been chiseled from stone, down to his belt, where a sword hung in its sheath. On the sash were words that seemed to be embroidered with fire, and it was clear that her first impression was wrong. The rider was not swathed in a white halo; he radiated light.

He *was* the light.

With masterful unconcern, the white rider reined in the powerful creature that continued stamping its hooves, then let itself be calmed, willing and obedient under his master's hand. At its shoulders, the horse stood several heads higher than a man, with rippling muscles that seemed carved from lightning. Its black eyes flared as if they had live coals inside. The canter down from the mountain peak had raised fine beads of perspiration—if that's what it could be called—for pricks of fire ran in little trickles down its flanks. The horse shook its mane, and sparks flew into the dewy grass around Mary's feet, where they sputtered and went out.

Mary broke the transfixed silence. "There was a man who led me to this place. He was—helping me. I don't know where he went, though. Do you have any idea where I can find him?" It sounded foolish, considering the circumstances, but she didn't know what else to say.

A look crossed the white rider's face as if he couldn't decide whether to weep or laugh. In a low tone, he said, *"Mary."*

And her eyes were opened.

The hunter's guise, in which he'd appeared to her on the other side of the water, was only one facet of this one who was now most radiantly revealed. For now she saw him as he really was.

Her guide.

Her wooer.

The healer of her soul.

The one who had saved her from the cold wind of death.

Leaning forward in the saddle, he let out a gentle sigh and said, "Receive me in your deepest heart of hearts."

At his words, a breeze sprang up, wafting warmly about her hair and dress. And to Mary's amazement, it actually raised her from the ground, bearing her up and toward him.

She had not known, until that very moment when she was filled and set a-course, that her soul had always been a limp-hanging sail, wanting wind and a way home.

The rider's arms were open to receive her, and she settled easily upon the saddle, where he encir-

cled her with his strength. Then he smiled at her—
a smile that could bring stars, moon and sun to
their knees, weeping for joy.

Sensing the gladness of its master, the horse
gave a mighty shiver.

The rider flicked at the reins and, with no more
than that, the horse seemed to clearly understand
his master's will. It turned its head back toward
the mountain and began to walk slowly.

Wherever they went, along the stream, the rising land was a-rush with whisperings, as if a great
secret were passing by.

Mary noticed something else. With the dawning
of honesty, time or some inner sense of balance had
finally righted itself. New she felt as if she had
found her way to reality.

Mary was overawed by all of this, and was thinking of how this open expanse was exactly the re-
verse of the funneling darkland, back in the mir-
ror-world she'd just escaped, where an angry storm
had nearly swallowed her into blackness.

"You have so many questions," the rider said
gently as they crossed the greening meadows. He
said it not as a rebuke but as an invitation.

Leaning against him, feeling both timid and
comforted, Mary found she wasn't at all surprised
that he knew her thoughts.

"I hate to admit it—seeing you. Being with you,"
she responded quietly. "But it's true. I don't understand so much of what's happened to me—before I came here and after."

"Ask whatever you will."

"It was you who spoke to me in my thoughts when I was trapped in the cave, wasn't it? I recognized the voice again as soon as you spoke just now. But you seemed so terrifying to me over there. And you're so different now. Why?"

"Before we passed through the water," the rider replied, "you were full of shadows and fears. Some were of your own imagination. Some came because certain lies about me were planted in you.

"Because you looked at things through fears and lies, you believed I wanted to hurt you. Then every word I said, every move I made toward you came as a threat. I could only keep my distance and lead you where I wanted you to go—except in the most extreme moments."

That reminded Mary of the foggy encounter in the pine grove, when she'd thought he set a death trap. Now it was clear he'd kept her from danger. So he had been influencing her along.

"Even when you were there to save me, I thought you were hunting for me because you wanted to hurt me," she admitted. "That makes me feel foolish—and ashamed."

He smiled. "Don't feel that way. I *was* hunting for you then. That's why you saw me in that form. But I'm a compassionate hunter, a good hunter, and I understood your fear. Like a wounded animal in a trap, you did not realize that I wanted to free you. You didn't understand me then. And even the way you see me now is the way you need to see me for the time being. It's all right—I am a prince, after all, as well as a hunter."

Mary was relieved. But one particular thing he'd said made her thoughtful.

"About the lies you mentioned," she probed. "You mean the things Michael told me about you. Isn't that right? It's odd. He never really accused you directly. He just said things that played on my own fear. That's how the lies worked. I can see that. But Michael wasn't his name, was it?"

"No. I won't speak his real name, not on a morning like this. And I think you know what it is."

They rode on in a tender silence. And after a time he said, "You have deeper questions."

Mary was hesitant at first. Then she asked, "Why didn't you come for me sooner? When I was small and alone and I needed you?"

"I was there all along," he replied.

On hearing this, she lifted her face and looked at him directly, wanting to object. But gazing into the curious light of his eyes was like looking through clear stones, and she found herself seeing reflections that caused her jaw to drop. Through his eyes she saw . . .

———————

. . . Oliver's lined face, alight with a patient smile of soft, giving, caring love.

The face of a Sunday school teacher, doctor and father—welcoming, offering kindnesses, doctoring her, teaching her truth, praying for her—every moment burning with the true concern of a daddy's love.

The fiercely loyal, challenging and accepting

love that radiated from the face of Olivia.

The face of a skinny, smiling boy, who had grown into the quiet, self-possessed confidence of manhood—and whose friendship still shone pure and clear after all these years, when the muscled, handsome heroes and posing artists had used her and gone.

And in all their faces burned a reflection of the intense flame of love that flared and shaped into the face of one man—who now encompassed her in his arms.

———

"Do you understand what I've shown you now?" the white rider asked. "Every act of love, no matter how small or common it looks to you, has only one true starting point. Love does become imperfect and incomplete when it flows through one person to another—anybody with an overly critical eye can see that. But—I've enabled you to see with new eyes. Now you can see that all love comes from me.

"There is a flaw in earthly loves, though—I want you to see this clearly. Few follow the path to the well of my love that runs deep and pure, because the way seems too dark, and because they are afraid of facing the lie that is buried in themselves, just as you were afraid. So they are always hungry inside, never content, trying to feed on and even devouring one another. What I am telling you is that love is really the tender half of truth—and without truth there is no freedom to love."

If Mary were not resting against him, these

glimmers of inner dawning would have shattered her. On one hand, she'd traded her soul for a ghastly thing that was no more than sickening self-love. And on the other, she had undervalued the common gifts of love that had been offered to her every day.

Mary was overwhelmed, appalled. "I was so blind."

She was silent for a time. With the horse's increased stride, they were already halfway to the silver forest.

"You have another question," the rider said, at length. "An angry question you've carried for a long time. I can feel it beating in your heart as you're leaning against me."

"Yes," she said, still hesitant, not knowing how to word it. "I don't understand about Uncle Wallace. Why he—why you—"

"Why he was allowed to hurt you?" he finished for her.

She nodded. "I was afraid to ask."

"You don't have to be afraid to ask anything at all—as long as you're willing to accept an answer that has more than one side to it. I'll tell you as much as you can understand for now."

Mary wasn't sure what he meant by "for now" but she listened intently.

"A moment ago you were appalled at how blind you'd been," he began. "It's worse than that. You've been foolishly romantic."

"I don't understand," she replied.

"First," he replied, "you were romantic in the

way you wanted the world to be. You wanted it to be heaven. But the world isn't heaven. Pain and real suffering are unavoidable.

"Because of that, you became angry at me when you were wounded. Even though you were told, 'In the world you'll have trouble.' Even though I said, 'Come to me when you're hurt and I'll place my love within you. Then you'll become strong enough to overcome every wound, even the sting of death.'

"You wanted another kind of prince to come for you—one who would prevent anything hurtful from ever happening at all," he said. "Don't feel embarrassed, it's true of most people. It's not wrong to want a world without pain, and the time for that is coming—but not yet."

Mary said, thinking out loud before she realized all that she was admitting, "I do remember those things you said now. But I grew up thinking they were nice Sunday school promises. I guess I never took those words to heart."

"You never took my words *into* your heart," he corrected. "If you had, they would have become as much a part of you as the bread you eat. You would have found that I was the light within you, bone of your bone and flesh of your flesh. You'd have looked out on life through my eyes, a little, even then."

Mary felt as though pieces of a great mystery were being set out before her, and that it would all finally make sense if she pondered it awhile.

"For now," he finished, "it's enough for you to hear me say this much plainly: I didn't send your pain, though I allowed enough of it to keep driving you until you came to me. And even at the end, I let you choose whether you'd come to me or not. Others stole your dignity by forcing and tricking you. I let you choose."

The horse continued its spirited gait, and as they neared the silver trees, the anthem Mary had been hearing grew louder. It was real, not imagined. She recognized it as the sweet sound of small children, their voices carried down on the clear air from the mountainside.

The horse knew the way under the forest's first boughs, still following the stream, and just inside the trees they came to a place that seemed familiar—a richly green lowland clearing. Here hundreds of yet-unblooming spikes of larkspur thrust up through the moist earth. In the center of it, one tall tree rained white petals, which fell and settled like tiny boats on a small pool cupped in a large rock.

Another mirror-image: Mary recognized the marsh she had come through at the end of the dying forest—only now it was transformed, returning to life.

Unexpectedly, the rider swung Mary down from the horse. Now, looking up at him again, she noticed the words emblazoned on his sash: *Faithful and True*. And she could faintly hear the words of the anthem:

> Who is she,
> appearing like morning?
> Fair as the moon,

clear as the sun,
majestic as the stars
in procession?

Who is she
coming up from the wilderness,
leaning on
the one she loves?

The rider raised his voice and called loudly in response:

She was
my wounded one—
the one my heart
longed for!

Nothing could withstand me
in my hunt,
not even the thorned
dark ways of her heart
where she ran from me
in pain.

Until the dawn breaks,
until the shadows flee away—
I have searched for her.

Like a signal, the rider's voice stopped the children's anthem at once, and from above came an army of miniature thunderclaps—the noise of running feet clamoring and pelting headlong down the slopes.

And then, even at a distance, Mary picked out one small voice among all the others—calling like a lamb that had lost its mother.

"Oh, please," she said, her heart leaping with both longing and dread, "if there's any other kind of reckoning, I can face it. But not this."

His face was kind and sorrowful but firm. "You know that I won't force you. But if you want to continue on with me, this is the one thing you have to do."

Bright faces were appearing—by dozens, by hundreds, by thousands and thousands—running breakneck toward them through the trees.

"All right," said Mary, tearing the answer from her heart. "But please don't leave me."

"I won't leave you," he said as he withdrew just a short distance, to the edge of the trees. There the army reached him, surrounding their champion. The innocents. The sacrificed unborn.

They thronged the horse, who patiently lowered its head so countless small hands could rub its nose. They pressed around the white rider, who stooped low to touch and bless the cowlicked, braided and tousled heads.

But in the throng, Mary saw just one face. In the clamor, she heard only one voice.

The rider looked down at this small blond head, said something, and nodded toward Mary. And then the child came timidly and alone into the clearing, looking with curious and cautious eyes.

Mary's heart was crushing. *How did I know her hair would be the color of mine?*

The little girl came and stood in front of her—not a baroque cherub, but a real child, with unusually green eyes and dirty bare feet. She was close enough to touch.

Mary sank to her knees. But the hands that ached to touch her child could not move.

"Are you still mad at me?" the little girl asked quietly, as if she were coming home from school after a difficult send-off just that morning.

"Mad at you?" Mary trembled. "Oh, no. Never. I thought you'd be mad at me, though. You have a right to be. I wasn't—good to you."

The little girl considered. "They're good to me here. I like it here. Are you going to stay with us now?" she asked hopefully.

"Not now, I think," said Mary, surprising even herself. Something the rider said had been coming clear.

"Oh," said the child, quietly, drawing with one toe in the grass. "Well, then, can you play with me?"

Mary was brimming with hope. "Yes. I will. If—if you'll let me just hold you first."

So matter-of-factly that it might have been something she'd done every day for years, the little girl shrugged and climbed onto Mary's lap. Suddenly she threw her arms around Mary's neck and squeezed, saying, "You can have a big hug."

It was Mary who hung on a long while, as tears that should have been wept were wept. She buried her face in the child's hair, loving the warm smell of it. And the little girl kept hugging her back, letting herself be held, until the ache in Mary's chest subsided.

"Are we going to play now?" the child prodded.

Then hand in hand, they searched the grassy clearing for flowers. Finding the larkspur, the child peeled back the green from the buds, pretending the stalks were dolls with faintly purple faces. Beside the small pool of water, they played a simple pretending game. Mary could not keep herself from reaching up to brush a few wandering strands of blond hair from the child's eyes.

Playfully, giggling, the little girl reached her fingers into the rocky pool. Then she threw her hand up, showering Mary with a sprinkling of white petals and water. Mary laughed and splashed her back.

"I love you, Mommy," said the child earnestly.

"And I love you, my darling," said Mary.

Too soon, it seemed, the time of love and play and absolution was over.

The woods had become quiet. All the other children had left. Only the white rider remained, astride the horse, waiting at a respectful distance.

As Mary approached, a look passed between the rider and the little girl. To Mary he said, "Where is your accuser now?"

"What do you mean?"

"When I set you down here, your heart was still accusing you," he replied. "If you hadn't let her come, you would have kept on accusing and condemning yourself as long as you live. There would always have been that much distance between us. I don't want it that way. I want you close to me. So, does your heart condemn you now?"

Mary searched inside herself.

Inwardly, she felt white as petals, clear as clean water washed with sunlight. At last it seemed the long night of her soul was over.

"No," she answered him, amazed. "Not condemned—not at all."

He was beaming triumphantly. "I want you always to remember how good this feels. It will make you want to stay close to me, even when your heart tries to lead you away from me again."

Mary turned to say something to the child, but she had gone back up the mountain.

"It was better for you not to see her go," he said reassuringly. "Goodbye means nothing where she lives. She wouldn't have known what you were saying. And now you know you'll see her again."

Before, Mary would have found this hard to accept. Now, surprisingly, she knew only peace.

"I never thought it was possible to feel so completely happy," she said meekly. Tears slipped freely down her cheeks.

He looked at her with mock severity. "I warned you, when you were hiding in those silly vines way back at the foot of the ravine, that you'd wish you hadn't run from me."

He reached down and lifted her in his arms again, then flicked the horse's reins.

"Hold on to me. I've been saving something for you."

One

What followed was a delirious gambol. The horse took his own lead, thundering up and into the forest glens. And where his feet flashed, a spring tide, which had been straining toward this very moment, let loose at last to wash the woods and widen in a wake of greenings and growings.

Trees stretched their waking limbs. On branch above and bush below, buds spun open like children's pinwheels at a fair. The overgrown, twisting mesh of wood rose and wild berry controlled itself into stems white with blossoms. Wild apples pinked, redbuds paraded up the hills, tulip trees turned out in orange and yellow; small anemones raised flutter-handed praise, lady-slippers arched serenely, and violets purpled in secret moss-grown grottoes.

The whole, rolling forest shimmered with new colors, the air scented with touches of innocent perfumes.

"This is our morning, Mary," the white rider whispered, as the horse carried them to the edge of a woodland clearing, which had become a bower of tulip poplars.

She knew the spot immediately. It was the clearing where she had crept up to spy on the hunter. Here he had subtly wooed her, whispering to her soul of his hunt for one who was bent on running from true love.

Now, brought close to his heart, she heard the words clearly, differently, as he sang them to her this time:

> His fingers hold the cold wind;
> in his hands, the killing frost.
> Where he walks, the ground is red—
> a trail of blood,
> a trail of blood.
>
> She will run before her hunter,
> faltering like the doe at dawn,
> She will suffer thorn and briar—
> without hope—
> without hope.
>
> He will seek her in the dark heart
> of her wild and haunted places.

Mary understood about the wounded doe, running from a relentless hunter who would bring healing. There still was quite a bit, however, that she didn't understand at all. And now, with nothing between them, nothing left to make her ashamed or embarrassed, she wasn't afraid to tell him so.

"The first part of that really scared me—about killing frost, and blood. It still sounds so gruesome. It's frightening, even though I know better. What does it mean?"

"It's the kind of love song you never hear in the world. I'll explain it all better in a moment," he smiled. "But first, I've been keeping something here for you. The best for last, you could say."

The horse stepped inside the bower of full-blossomed tulip trees. And though no one at all was within light-years or dimensions of this spot, the trees seemed to close ranks and fold their arms, standing sentry.

Within the woodland chapel, the white rider bent close and whispered in her ear, his breath warm against her hair, a name by which she would be known to him, and which no one on earth would ever know.

And there was a gift: The woods surrounding this secret place was drenched with diamond lights.

Awed and humbled and dazzled, Mary accepted into her open heart the one thing that the whole universe of created beings cries out for.

Then, at the rider's silent command, the horse cantered out from under the circling trees.

Someone watching nearby would have blinked and wondered if they were seeing two passing brightnesses or only one as they wound a lingering way through the lower forest. The horse wanted to swallow immense distances with strides like lightning but allowed his power to be checked for the sake of his master and the radiant soul he bore.

The rider reached out and broke off a long whip of wood rose, heavy with fragrant unfolding petals and dark-green leaves, and also covered with tiny spikes. Deftly, he wove it into a circlet. And before Mary could pull away, he set it upon her head.

To her surprise, it did not prick or hurt her at all.

"You see?" he said. "Nothing can really harm you now. Unless you change yourself into an instrument of harm, nothing can ever harm you again."

The horse was given his way once more, and they left the lower forest behind. In a blaze of leaps, the magnificent creature carried them up to a mountain meadow at the foot of a ravine. From higher up came the rushing sound of a waterfall, and below them spread a vast panorama—exactly the same, yet completely changed from when Mary had last looked out upon it.

"What do you see?" he asked.

She saw spring. Green, yellow, purple, pink, living spring. The great bowl of forest, open land, and, beyond that, the far-off crystal sea, were alive, leaping and alight with it. Spring had come at last for Mary, for she'd been judged "worthy of life."

Across the sea, the storm had subsided. Even the oily darkness had dissipated. What she saw now was a land spread over with a deadening blanket of ice. The reflection of crimsoning lights—the light from this world of eternal beauty, shining across into that other world—fell even brighter in the storm's wake.

"You wanted to know about the first part of my song. The part that sounded gruesome," the rider said. "The wind and killing frost were in my hands. Your friend Michael was hoping they'd catch up with you. That's why he tried to waylay you in the thick woods. And when that didn't work, he led you into traps. I was always behind you, holding back the full consequences of your wrong choices."

"And the trail of blood?" Mary asked.

"By now you know whose blood was meant," he said, smiling. "Not yours."

Beyond the dividing waters, the white iciness was anointed and sealed, all of it, in the blood-red color of the light above it. From this vantage point it looked entirely different. Beautiful.

"All that was taken from you," the rider said quietly, "was taken not for your harm, but that you might seek it in my arms. All that you mistook as lost I have kept for you here. But it's not for you to invite the hand of death."

"The hand of death," Mary repeated. The immensity of it all was too great. "What would have happened if I had chosen to stay on that black shore?" she asked.

"You'd been listening to lies for a long time. They'd taken a strong hold, so that you were starting to become a shadow. Do you remember feeling faint and soul-sick? If you had chosen him, you would have become his bride. A shadow bride."

Mary was searching for some last, lost detail, still vague in her recollection. Ignoring this, she said with satisfaction. "I just knew this was heaven."

"Heaven?" he said abruptly. "No, not yet." He turned so they were facing each other. "It's true, you were on a course with death. But the course has been reversed. I wanted you to understand so that you can tell others."

When she looked uncertain, he added, "Tell them that memory doesn't have to be a prison of the past. If you place every darkness you've suffered into my hands, and even your own evil choices, I will make them a path leading you to deeper life—and to the work you have yet to do."

A sudden rush of longing came over Mary. "You're sending me back, aren't you?"

He held her close, to help her accept his words. "Not back. There's no such thing as going back. You're going on. This is only a place behind the world you know—a place of reckoning—just as you were told. That much was true, though he used it to his own advantage."

Mary started to object, but thunder broke around her as the horse thrust upward into the wide mouth of the ravine. Trees parted to let them pass and stone walls narrowed on either side. The stream led them into the ravine's funnel to a brightly churning pool at the bottom of a rocky drop.

Then Mary's stomach did a sickening dip as the horse took the rocky challenge in one majestic leap.

And in that moment, she saw to her amazement that the roaring waterfall beside them was reversed. It was rushing *up* the cliff!

Beside three stalwart evergreens at the top edge, the horse came to rest. Giving a satisfied flick of its tail, it scattered flaming shards of light like shining glints from shaken silver foil.

And there awaiting her at the top of the cliff lay the still-frozen edge of the traffic circle in downtown Washington. The stream flowed back into pavement, and on the other side, the small park was a gray still-life, just as she'd seen it on that April afternoon. But as they watched, everything was starting to green and waken in slow motion.

"You have a long climb ahead of you yet, before the day breaks," said the white rider. She started to object, but he prevented her from speaking. "I don't want you to feel any regrets about going on from here. So I'll let you have one last look."

Mary was feeling dizzy from the last spurt and leap of their climb—and almost sick to her stomach again. The idea of "a long climb ahead" wasn't appealing. When the rider pointed up toward the mountain peak, however, her eyes followed.

The emerald rainbow rested like a diadem above. Behind the peak, the light of an eternal, unsetting sun seemed as eager to wash over this side of the mountain as the straining forest buds had been. But that was not what drew Mary's attention.

In a meadow just below the emerald glow, like glittering gems on a felt-like greensward, she saw a multitude of people. Among them, three stood waving. Mary knew them even at a distance, though two looked much younger than she remembered them. There were Oliver and Lucille and, at their side, a little girl.

Mary turned quickly to the rider with a question in her eyes.

"I know what you want to ask," he said. "But Lucille's story is as sacred as your own. We have a secret, too, she and I. You have no idea what she suffered—things that no one ever knew."

Suddenly, Mary was wrapped in a final embrace.

Then strong hands were setting her down from the horse, and her feet lighted on one branch of the frozen stream—or rather, on pavement that was thawing, and slippery.

Mary felt herself slipping from the rider's grasp.

"But why here? Why bring me back here?"

"Sometimes in your life I allow pain—so that you'll always remember what you learn as you go through it. At this place, in time, you were choosing death. Now go, and choose life."

She was struggling not to fall, catching one last glimpse of his shining face as he said, "I've shown you things in the light. Hold on to them in the darkness. And never forget to look for me."

The park scene spun out of slow motion. Mary felt herself slipping, off-balance, her stomach tense with nausea.

A young woman, familiar and yet a stranger . . .

———

. . . was seated on one of the benches at Dupont Circle, the April sun falling warm upon her hands and face. Inwardly there was only a misery of creeping cold.

In the four weeks since the abortion, she'd suffered torturing dreams over and over in which she fought through a tangled wilderness, trying to escape from a brooding, stalking force. Always, she came to a sea of dark waters and looked down to see a small, pale, drowned face.

She would waken to her own screams.

A dozen times she tried to phone or see Mitch. At his apartment there was no answer. At his art gallery she was blocked by a smart, pretty, dark-haired young man who identified himself as Mitch's new assistant. Despite her persistence, he fended her off: Mitch was busy—there were problems arranging a new show, requiring an emergency trip to the west coast. He'd see that Mitch got her message.

Finally she'd insisted he meet her today, at lunchtime. And he was late. Panic wanted to erupt from the floor of her soul. Breathing deeply, she steadied herself by focusing on the watery voice of the fountain, but she could not escape an awful sense that she was just a bit player in a soap opera, one who was about to be written out of the script.

A little blond girl in a pink pinwale dress toddled by, cradling a porcelain-faced doll. "See my baby?" she said, fixing Mary with a direct, green-eyed gaze.

Mary gripped the edge of the bench to keep from

bolting like a crazy woman. Feeling ill, she closed her eyes.

Someone tapped her shoulder. It was not Mitch, but the young assistant. He had apparently doused himself with some kind of expensive cologne, so the appeal of it was ruined by the overkill. "Are you okay? You don't look well."

"Where's Mitch?" she asked desperately. "Why isn't he here?"

"Well, we've gotten into some new stuff at the gallery. Mitch phased out the Caribbean garbage. He doesn't stay into any one thing for too long. That's the way he is. I've turned him on to a few new artists. Some guys I know from San Francisco—"

"Where is he!" she shouted, cutting him off. "I need to talk to him. Why is he avoiding me?"

The young man looked at her soberly. "I'll give you some advice. I've known Mitch for a couple of years now. His moods change. One day you're in the spotlight—then he goes on to new things. If you know that about him, it's easier to take. That's just the way he is. And if he thinks you're closing him in, he's gone."

"You don't understand," she insisted. "I've got to see him . . . There's something that I did—it was for him."

"Look," said the young man, nervously backing off, "I only came to give you his regrets. The rest is between you two. I guess he'll call you if he wants to talk."

He couldn't get away fast enough, dodging his

way among the crowded lanes of circling traffic. Angry horns blared as he hurriedly wove across the street.

Then she saw him. There was no mistaking the aviator jacket. From a store-front doorway, where he'd obviously been watching, Mitch stepped out and clapped a hand on the young man's shoulder.

The two turned a corner and disappeared, never looking back.

Powerful surges seized her. Faces rose from within, staring . . .

Uncle Wallace.

Cam.

Mitch.

Mixing with the faces of other men whose love she'd hungered for, they congealed into one face. One darkly handsome stranger who beckoned her soul out into a wilderness, where death could overtake her.

Over beside the fountain, the little girl in the pink dress was being lifted in the arms of a large husky man in an elegantly tailored business suit. Laughing, he nuzzled his face lovingly into the tummy of her dress.

Mary felt only a creeping, numbing cold—felt lifeless as the fountain's stone-carved figures. In her chest a weight was crushing out her breath. She rose on weakening legs.

Maybe Mitch was right and Olivia was wrong. Olivia had said to listen for the voice of truth behind the lies. But maybe there was nothing beyond this mean, bitter world.

And then she bolted, running as if that world were ending, deliberately out into the line of speeding cars.

A horn blared. There was a bright flash, as of sun on glass . . . or on water. And a sickening impact. . . .

"Mary?"

She swam up into consciousness, toward the faint sound of a familiar voice.

Her head was bandaged and felt twice its size, and her eyes winced at the light streaming through the hospital window. Every bone and muscle ached. One hand was strapped to a bedrail, with tubes of clear fluid running down to it.

Olivia, standing beside her, was looking down, her dark eyes peering into Mary's face with concern, surprise, and hope.

Mary smiled weakly and tried to speak. A tube prevented her.

"Don't try to say anything," Olivia said eagerly. "Just rest. I won't leave you. We've taken turns staying with you since—since the accident. When you're out of here, you're coming home with Harlan and me for a while."

Mary shut her eyes momentarily. And opened them again when something warm splashed against her hand.

Olivia was closer, leaning over her, weeping.

"You've been in a coma, Mary. For more than a week. It's the first of May," she explained, gently stroking Mary's cheek with one finger.

"Two days ago we nearly lost you," she said with fresh tears. "We knew you were losing the fight. I was sitting right here beside you, holding your hand, and I felt you slip away from me, Mary. The doctors and nurses worked for a long time, and they were ready to give up." Her voice choked with emotion.

Mary was only half hearing all this. She was fighting with pain. Not just physical pain—that was bearable—but with a fearful question. She was staring at a tree outside her window, some sort of purple-leafed ornamental that was dropping its faded petals.

Was it only a dream? she thought remorsefully. *Would he leave me like this?*

Immediately an inner voice was present with her, whispering, *Don't you know me, Mary? I'm here forever. I was with you, and now I'll be in you.*

A movement drew Mary's attention. Someone had joined Olivia beside the bed. She expected to see Harlan, but this was someone else. A tall, sandy-haired someone who smiled down at her tenderly, his deep-set eyes filled with kindness and concern.

Olivia wiped her eyes with the back of one hand. "Walker's been here with me most of the time. He was down in the chapel praying for you when he heard the emergency call. They were going to quit, but he made them try one more time."

"Someone sent you back to us," said Walker.

Mary smiled at both of them through the pain. Smiled, because their love was a gift far greater than she deserved—and because of the other gift that was still present, set within her heart forever, pure and white and shining like a precious stone.

Acknowledgments

The initial spark of inspiration for Mary's story came while listening to Terry Talbot perform his intensely powerful song "Face to Face," which drove the vision into my mind of the return of Christ, in the clouds, with the millions of murdered unborn safe at his side. Thank you, Terry.

Many thanks to Dr. William Backus and to Leanne Payne, whose writings have greatly influenced my life and this work.

Gratitude beyond words goes to Peggy Anderson for being unsparing in love, unsparing in honesty. And to Larry Cochran, one of the finest, most faithful men of prayer I have ever known, for his vision of the white rider's fiery horse—which I have imbued with the patient strength I so often see in my friend. And to Dr. Carol Currier, for words that gave me launch: "You've been given a story that will bring healing to many."

Most of all, thanks to the friend and brother who stuck with me in the wilderness of a long winter's writing.

DAVID HAZARD was trained in the art of story-telling by such gifted writers as the late Catherine Marshall and her husband, Len LeSourd, and the writing team of John and Elizabeth Sherrill. He has won several writing awards, co-authored the international bestseller *No Compromise: The Life Story of Keith Green*, and teaches international writing schools. This is his first novel.

When he is not administrating a private, editorial-development service, editing or writing, he enjoys outdoor sports with his family.

In the foothills of northern Virginia's Blue Ridge Mountains, he makes his home, together with his wife, MaryLynne, and their three children, Aaron, Joel and Sarah Beth.